T0343800

PENGUIN BOOK

## JUVENILES AND OTHER STORIES

Apinuch Petcharapiracht (also known under the pen name 'Moonscape') is a Chinese-Thai writer who leads a peaceful life with her cat and dog in Phetchaburi, Thailand. Now that the marriage equality bill has been passed in Thailand, she hopes to finally live her dream of marrying her girlfriend. She wrote *Juveniles and Other Stories* based on her grim memories from her childhood that have been buried and left unforgotten for one and a half decades.

ALSO BY

*Death and the Maiden* (2024)

# Juveniles and Other Stories

Apinuch Petcharapiracht
*Translated from* Thai by
Kornhirun Nikornsaen

PENGUIN BOOKS
An imprint of Penguin Random House

PENGUIN BOOKS

Penguin Books is an imprint of the Penguin Random House group of
companies whose addresses can be found at global.penguinrandomhouse.com

Published by Penguin Random House SEA Pte Ltd
40 Penjuru Lane, #03-12, Block 2
Singapore 609216

First published in Penguin Books by Penguin Random House SEA 2025

*Juveniles & Other Stories* includes elements that might not be suitable
for some readers. It contains unsettling themes, depictions of violence, instances
of sexual content involving minors, and mentions of child sexual abuse.
Readers who may be sensitive to these elements please take note.

ISBN 9789815204896

Typeset in Lora by MAP Systems, Bengaluru, India

www.penguin.sg

# Contents

# Juveniles

## 1

**I met him for the first time when I was eight.**
'Playing hide-and-seek? Want me to help?'

He was a child from the same village, from the large house at the end of the alley whose occupants, as I heard, wanted nothing to do with others.

'Go hide in the storm drain, I'll close the lid for you. No one's going to open it, and there's no water in the drain—it hasn't been used for so long.'

I had just joined the children's bicycle gang at that time. We, elementary school children, would play simple games like variants of the border-crossing game, football, or sepak takraw. On that day, our gang leader suggested that we play hide-and-seek—there was no one around the garbage dump area except for us, and I had never been good at hiding, so I was always among the first ones to be found.

Then, I met him: a boy around my age with the palest skin and the scariest pair of eyes that I had ever seen. His eyes were as black as a deep pond.

'Who are you? What's your name?'

He answered my question while he was lifting the lid of the storm drain.

1

'My name is Hai Saeng.'

Then, all lights were robbed. I lay still in a dried-up storm drain that was once dug to prevent flooding, listening to the sound of my friend running around, finding others in hiding, one after the other. That was the first time they couldn't find me. The thought made my heart thump with glee, but soon after, their voices went quiet.

They had already stopped seeking.

I was becoming uneasy while trying to push the lid open. Sadly, a cement lid, half a metre in width, was too heavy for an eight-year-old. I only learned later that not only did Hai Saeng close the lid, but he also dragged a planting pot from a nearby house to add more weight on top of it, hence the reason I couldn't push it open, no matter how hard I tried. However, with a pot of fiddle-leaf fig standing so out of place and out of the ordinary, the grown-ups and rescue team finally found me around one o'clock in the morning, before I became dehydrated or overheated and passed out. Mom cried a river, forbade me from playing with the bicycle gang ever again, then proceeded to hurl insults and yelled about those good-for-nothing kids that left me alone to the point that they started crying. They said, hiccupping, that they thought I had gone home already, since they really couldn't find me. I didn't blame them—and Mom's rants worked, as their parents forbade them from playing with me ever again too.

As for the true culprit, I didn't mention him.

At that time, I wasn't even sure if he really existed.

## 2

The second time we met, I was riding my bicycle past his house alone.

'Well, were you scared?'

He grabbed on to the wrought iron gate, beamed at me, and asked, without guilt, about the event that had haunted me for a week with sleepless nights. Still, I mustered up courage and answered, 'It was fun.'

'Fun?' Hai Saeng's eyes shone. 'Is it? How was it? Tell me.'

'How about you try going down there yourself?'

'If I do, it'll be a boring game, since no one's going to look for me.'

*He has no friends*, I thought. I had never seen him talking to anyone in the village before—actually, I had never seen him anywhere at all.

'What about your parents?'

'They aren't around,' Hai Saeng replied coolly, inserting a huge key into the keyhole and taking off the chain that locked the iron gates in place. He smiled. 'You want to come in?'

I hurriedly grabbed on to my bicycle's handlebar.

'Don't force yourself if you're scared.' Hai Saeng laughed and headed back towards his house, leaving the door ajar just so. Had he no fear of burglars at all?

I looked around. The eerie atmosphere was complete with deep green mosses and vines crawling on the ground, windows sunken into the house, and an entry door that was situated exactly right in the middle—such that it gave off the look of a mouth of a cave. I doubted any burglars would dare cross its threshold—by simply observing it, I could almost see it gobbling up humans. In spite of all this, I parked my bicycle there and followed him inside hesitantly.

Hai Saeng's house was as quiet and damp as a demon's lair. In the middle of the house, at the demon's heart, was an upright piano.

'That's Mother's,' Hai Saeng said.

'Your mom plays piano?'

'Used to.' He smiled. *Can you, then?* I wanted to ask him, but I didn't. Hai Saeng simply said, 'Come,' and brought me around to take a look at other parts of the house—all of which were as dark as night. The luxurious furnishing pieces were all spotlessly clean yet lifeless, and withered flowers were left in a dried-up vase. How long had his parents been away? Was there no one beside him? 'Who took care of you, and what did you eat . . .' I swarmed him with questions, none of which Hai Saeng replied to. He opened a fridge, and we were greeted with heaps of food. There were housekeepers taking care of daily necessities for him, but they barely made themselves known, as if they needed to remain hidden.

With no other children in the village to hang out with, I spent my whole semester break with Hai Saeng. He *played* like no other. Hai Saeng didn't have a bicycle, didn't play football, and cared not for physical sports. I had him ride on the back of my own bicycle. He stood on the footrests and refused to sit down, his finger pointing us to wherever he wanted to explore: groves, snake nests by the river bank, and the deserted makeshift shack of a homeless man alike. 'Dao Nhue, do you dare steal the tobacco he's hidden away?' he dared. At first, I was against it and only replied with, 'No, let's not'. But he brought it up whenever he had the chance. 'Do you think we should bring something back as proof we came here?' he asked when we were riding past a Thai chess table next to an empty local grocer.

'What would you need that for?' I jabbed him in the ribs and tried dragging him away from those freaky ideas. Hai Saeng smiled and bent down to whisper next to my ear, his cold breath tickling it.

A *secret hideout*.

I had no idea what he was talking about, yet I, regardless, stole a red horse piece from the box with no one noticing. And that was the first time I ever stole anything.

### 3

A horse chess piece, a stainless steel bowl from a shaved ice shop, a short stump of a candle from the temple, loose change from a beggar's bowl, a moulted snakeskin from the riverside, a dead clock from a drawer in Mom's desk, plastic rope from a spotted dove's nest, a strip of fabric that was once tied to shrines and rotting trees, what remained of butterfly wings, wooden chopsticks, a rusty doorknob—our *secret hideout* was soon filled with useless knick-knacks that we had borrowed from strangers without ever asking.

Hai Saeng was the one who had found the place incidentally. It was a hole made of dry grass next to the Phetchaburi River that was the perfect size for two children to take cover. We pushed its roof higher up, supported it with a large branch, and began decorating the inside with the treasures we had gathered. We crawled inside, tried to lay down, and pretended as if it was a magnificent castle all the while feeling grassy itches all over our bodies. There was a moment where I wondered why we even bothered with creating such a house, what with Hai Saeng's house being much more palatial. While I was lost in thought, I spied Hai Saeng, who was lying beside me, looking my way. In one fleeting moment, he smiled. His pale skin, bathed in the sun that shone in ripples through our roof made of twigs, turned him into something illusory. Like a spirit. Like a *ghost*. I reached out, unknowingly, to touch his face. He didn't turn away but rather tilted his head closer in, saying, 'This is a secret hideout just for us alone, do you understand?'

We went there every day throughout the summer. We would take our shoes off and wade through water reaching up to our ankles with our feet sinking into mud. On some days, we wouldn't lounge in the grassy shack, but instead sit on the edge of a bridge with me enjoying my bag of crisps that came with a spin top, and Hai Saeng eating his red-yellow ice lolly with green sugar coated on top. The hems of his pants were pulled up above his knees. I noticed that his clothes were much more concealing compared to children of the same age.

He never wore any tank tops or flip flops. Some days he would sit still, observing me as I ran around, catching small fish between my cupped hands and showing them to him. 'What kind of fish is this?' he asked. I told him I didn't know, then sparkles shone in his dark eyes. Hai Saeng reached a hand out, pinched the fish by its tail, and watched it struggle in the air.

'Open your mouth, Dao Nhue.'

'What are you doing?' I was concerned.

'I'm ordering you.' He smiled. I always did as he told me whenever he uttered that word. 'Close your eyes,' he continued. Then a smooth yet uncanny object was dropped into my mouth. It wriggled and had a taste of mud.

Hai Saeng had put the fish inside my mouth.

'Swallow,' he ordered again. I glared at him in protest but kept my mouth shut regardless and tried to swallow it as I was told. In the end, I couldn't do it. I turned around and spit the poor thing back into the river, looking at it as the fish spun around in confusion for a moment then swam away. Hai Saeng clicked his tongue in annoyance. But, believe me, he wasn't going to stop pestering me after such a small disappointment; and I, too, danced to his tune with no lessons learned.

I naively thought that everything would stay the same, and it did until the day Varuna let down his first wave of rain in May. We saw our riverside hideout sink underneath water. A huge mass of water took hold of such a vast area that it was impossible to move to the other side barefoot. The first day of school arrived, and I heard that Hai Saeng had to head back to Bangkok for school. His family had only bought that house as a temporary holiday home. When I rode my bicycle past that house after school, it was already empty.

That was all I knew: a summer that remained a secret between Hai Saeng and I. My life returned to days deemed normal by the common people, and I would let it remain so until he returned.

## 4

During the big school break after I finished sixth grade, I learned that he was back as I overheard some people talking about weird noises from the house at the end of the alley. 'That blaring piano sound in the night, why! Dogs were howling at the same time, and I couldn't bring myself to walk past it,' an old fortune teller told Mom. I overheard them talking upon returning home from a football match with friends on an artificial turf.

My friends from the elementary years headed separate ways in their academic pursuits. After our last end-of-semester exam, we bade goodbye to one another and swore to remain friends forever. We wrote on each other's uniform shirts with permanent pens and added heart-shaped stickers alongside. I promised them to treasure my shirt, only to find it hung on a drying rack the next morning, all the colours mixed into an unsightly shape. It was my mom's doing. She had thrown everything into the washing machine, followed by indigo dye powder and a good rub of bleach—completely forgetting that I had no more use of my elementary school uniforms.

Ink stains on that shirt faded away as quickly as our friendships from elementary days. I forgot about them within the course of the next few days. I never, however, forgot about that strange eight year old whom I had once met at the house at the end of the alley; I kept looking for him whenever I went past the riverbank. I would see the shadows of two children going inside that grassy shack, our feet soaked with mud, counting the clouds in the sky, that short moment where he gave me his smile under the shaded sun, me running after an ice cream truck for him, him plotting an evil plan and having me carry it out. Memories accompanied by the sound of the river continued to disturb me in my dreams, even when our hideout was already buried deep beneath, as if it had never existed in the first place.

I parked my bicycle in front of that house and rang the doorbell, my heart thumping as I heard the doorknob turn. It was Hai Saeng.

'Long time no see.'

Those were his first words.

'Hai Saeng.'

'Dao Nhue.'

We regarded each other silently for a long while. He, at ten years old, looked taller. His arms and legs stretched longer, yet fit, nonetheless. His cracking voice sounded smooth to the ears and not too coarse to suffocate one's senses. I even held my breath when he called my name. It's *different*. And then there were those one-of-a-kind eyes, as deep as a deep pond, their corners long and slim. 'Come on in,' he said. I made my way through the wrought iron gates as I once had four years ago. Everything looked much more aged. They had been away for so long.

'Did you come here to spend the semester break?' I asked.

'I came here to stay.' He smiled. 'I moved here to study—made it through the B School's entrance exam.'

It was the province's high school, whose entrance exam I had passed as well. I was surprised and asked about his parents.

'They're divorced. You didn't see them last time because they were separated, and I was shoved around as extra baggage.' Hai Saeng poured some juice into a glass and handed it to me. 'You don't have to worry though, I'm the only one living here now. Mother only sends someone to look after the house once in a while, and there's a driver to take me to school and back, then he's gone.'

He said it so casually, as if it had nothing to do with him. I felt a tingling pain listening to him. He still had no friends to play with. I invited him to play football with the group I hung out with. He shook his head and yawned, then told me that he had tutoring classes to attend.

I started talking about the past, that grassy shack, our secret hideout, our first steal and the next ones. 'Do you remember,' I said, 'that drunkard uncle was so pissed off when we took his fishing boat to row around.' Hai Saeng sat there listening to me. His cool smile was not as cheerful as when we were younger, yet it tugged at my heartstrings. I felt chills running up my body from down below. My speech was rushed and somewhat shaky from an unknown cause. 'You said that our shack was similar to a bowerbird's nest. I thought that you were so weird, but when I asked Dad to Google it for me, I found it exactly as you said.'

But Hai Saeng only replied cooly, 'That's nice. I don't remember much about those things any more.'

At that exact moment, it came to me that many things had indeed changed during the span of four years.

## 5

During junior high, we went to the same school while studying in different classes. Hai Saeng attended extra tutoring classes according to the schedule that his mother had arranged for him. I, on the other hand, did a myriad of extracurricular activities, so we rarely met in school apart from passing glances. We would greet one another with a simple nod and nothing more. He never had lunch at the canteen nor showed up at any internet café after school. Sometimes, while I was playing football with my friends, I would see him walking in the hallway on the third floor, surrounded by his new group of friends whom he turned around to talk to from time to time. He cast his gaze down at the grassy field. I might be thinking ahead of myself, but I thought he looked at me—whenever our eyes met, I would lose control of the football and shoot it at my team's goal, and he would laugh. He stood there observing for a while before his friend dragged him away.

I let it slip during dinner with my family and talked about him. Mom said that I should be more like Hai Saeng.

'Why don't you ask him for help with your studies?' She looked at my school report and furrowed her brows, then dragged me to Hai Saeng's house even though she had never met him before. She said to the pale-skinned boy in a pleading voice, 'My son's really bad at English, could you please help him with it, dear Saeng? Tell him to study more, we are neighbours after all.' *How embarrassing.* I avoided his gaze and mumbled to not take Mom's words to heart.

'Of course, Auntie.'

Hai Saeng replied in a voice that sounded so formal, one he had never used with me before, one which sounded like a dependable senior's, even with us being of the same age. My mom was over the moon. At that moment, I spied him winking at me while making a throat-slitting gesture with his finger.

Once a week, on the day he had no extra tutoring, I would drop by his class, M.1/1—*English Programme.* I read the sign in front of the class, pushed the wooden door open, and dragged him away from his friends. Hai Saeng's friends were surprised at first to see me bursting into the classroom, but they became more friendly towards me once I had Hai Saeng explain briefly to them—'This boy's mother doesn't want her son to repeat the year.' I made no sound of protest and looked at Hai Saeng as he typed away on his mobile phone, telling his driver to not pick him up that day.

Compared to when he had once stood on my bicycle's footrests as I drove him around, he had grown up much more. He stopped standing on the footrests and agreed to sit behind me on my motorbike. Hai Saeng didn't have a helmet, and I promised to find one for him. Hai Saeng looked at the people walking around the school, then he stretched his arms out, wrapped them around my waist, and buried his face into my back without care, others' gazes be damned. 'If I don't hold on tight, I will fall, right?' I knew that he did it with full intent. I felt his lips on my back as they curved into a smile—a most devilish smile.

## 6

'Dao Nhue, do you know that you're quite popular yourself?'

'Huh?'

'Do you know Ammy from my class? The one who was chosen to carry the pedestal tray on teacher's day.'

'Ah, yes, I saw her.'

'She likes you, mister footballer.'

This chit-chat took place in an ice cream parlour while we were studying English. Hai Saeng was having his chocolate sundae while overseeing me working on an English worksheet. He was a horrible teacher, to be honest. He would begin talking about stuff even with the exercise sheet being timed. And I couldn't possibly ignore him. I looked up after finishing the last multiple-choice question about grammatical errors. Hai Saeng had finished his ice cream by then. *People with a sweet tooth tend to be emotionally unstable*, I thought silently to myself. They are unpredictable, like raging storms, and do whatever they please.

'So?' Hai Saeng said as he began grading my exercise sheet. Nearly half of them were wrong.

'So?' I was confused.

'What do you think of Ammy?'

'Wait, it's weird that you're the one asking me this.'

'What, Dao Nhue? Isn't this the period of life where young men are driven by their libido?' he asked nonchalantly. I scratched my head awkwardly and answered, 'Don't talk as if you're already old.'

Hai Saeng laughed light-heartedly and continued grading my exercise. I observed his profile: his jawline, the shape of his nose, black hair with loose threads near his ears, thin eyelashes that weren't too long, the corners of his lips that crooked slightly upward as if to mock the other party, making him seem haughty yet attractive at the same time. I gulped. How could I possibly tell him that my libido-driven fantasy had no place for that Ammy he mentioned nor any other women in this world?

Ever since my hormones began working age-appropriately, I began having the same type of dreams as other teenagers my age. I saw us, both at our present height, lying on our sides in that riverside grassy shack, facing each other. Scattering sunlight graced Hai Saeng's pale body. He was in his school uniform. I took off his belt and touched his smooth skin underneath his clothes to prove that he was real. He moaned through his teeth with a voice that had begun cracking not too long ago. He wrapped his arms around my neck and softly cursed when I lifted his leg on to my waist. My index finger dragged downward, ridding him of the sock that once wrapped around his ankle, letting it fall slowly on to the ground next to us. I began kissing his ankles—

' . . . Nhue.'

'. . .'

'Dao Nhue.'

'Hmm, huh?'

I jolted, even if mildly. Hai Saeng pushed the exercise book towards me. 'You got only twenty-one problems out of fifty correct. You've improved slightly,' he said sarcastically. 'I agreed to help you with your study, and here you are, spacing out.'

'Oh, thanks.'

'What were you thinking about, huh?'

Hai Saeng stared right at me. I hurriedly searched for something else to cover up my wild imagination.

'So, what about you?'

'What about me?'

'Someone that you like. Do you have one?'

What was I expecting asking him such a question? Hai Saeng was surrounded with people who liked him, but his personal life was ever mysterious, and he didn't look like someone who would answer questions easily—which was true. He didn't answer. Instead, he narrowed his eyes, rested his chin on his elbow, and looked straight at me.

'Open your mouth, Dao Nhue,' he said out of the blue.

'What?'

'And close your eyes too.'

'Huh?'

I remembered the taste of living fish from the river right at that moment, but my body obeyed his order regardless. Was he preparing to punish me for spacing out during our study session? I kept my eyes closed for a long time while waiting for his divine punishment, all the while preparing myself mentally for the possibility that he would most likely shove some weird garbage, like the used tissues scattered on this table, into my mouth.

But the taste that graced my tongue was something numbingly sweet, juicy, and strange. I opened my eyes and found that the thing on my tongue was the maraschino cherry from Hai Saeng's sundae.

'Eat it up,' Hai Saeng said. I shut my lips around the cherry and began pulling its stem out as I began to chew it. Its stem was already tied into a knot.

'Wait.' I remembered something after I had already swallowed the cherry. 'How did you feed me this cherry just now?'

Hai Saeng smiled in satisfaction. He wove his fingers in front of him and laughed.

'Care to guess?'

## 7

My football friends called Hai Saeng 'that weird guy'—'You spend a lot of time with that weird guy from the EP class, don't you?'—and now that I think about it, Hai Saeng really stood out like a sore thumb in a rural school. He dressed according to the rules by the letter, and he was always smiling, yet hard to approach. His eyes always met with those of the one he was talking to, but the other party would feel as if he wasn't paying any attention to them. 'How arrogant.' 'He's a young master, don't you know?' 'I feel stupid talking to him, even when the guy doesn't say much himself.' Other boys from my class talked about him like that, their voices somewhat annoyed. As for the girls, they simply said that he was handsome and that was it. No one knew him beyond that. In conclusion, Hai Saeng attracted the attention of others in good and bad ways alike, what with him not doing anything in the first place, and I don't think he cared about that at all.

'We have been neighbours ever since we were young,' I gave them the briefest explanation. We only ever got close during that one summer when I was eight years old, and it was only for a span of two months. That much was true, but it was a piece of memory that I could announce with swelling pride—except for that part about how he trapped me in a drain at our first meeting.

During junior high, our friendship progressed slowly, unlike that fiery imagination burning in my chest. I met him once a week after school during that period of time when he gave me private English lessons without so much as a complaint. We moved the location of our class around from an ice cream parlour to a milkshake shop and even to his house. My mom was overjoyed whenever Hai Saeng agreed to hold the lesson at my house, but I wasn't too happy with that.

'Mom's noisy and needs attention. We should have studied at your place,' I grumbled. Hai Saeng shrugged, flopped down on my bed, and began reading comic books from my bookshelf without a care while having me work on my timed exercise. His body and his gestures disturbed me greatly. He rolled around on the bed in which I spent an unholy amount of time thinking of him. I believed he knew that, and that was why he often stole glances above the book my way.

'Focus,' he chided, and I hurriedly shifted my focus towards the exercise sheet. My score remained as unsatisfactory as always.

The semester break, on the other hand, was a period of time where we didn't get to meet each other at all. 'My mother signed me up for a tutoring course. I'll be back by the end of October,' he said as if the matter didn't concern him. I helped him pack his bag with the few personal items he had. 'I'll be staying at Mother's house in Bangkok, even if she doesn't want to see me that much.' Hai Saeng laughed. We bade each other a customary farewell in front of his house. 'Mother wants me to enter a well-known public high school.' I saw a shadow in that pair of empty eyes. His unconcerned facial expression annoyed me. *How long will you continue to live according to your mother's wishes? She doesn't care about you at all.* I could only clench my fists. Hai Saeng asked if I had anything else to say. I shook my head, knowing full well that I had no right to. There was nothing between us, and thus I could only look on—in a manner very similar to an obedient dog—as that luxury car drove him away.

The house at the end of the alley was left abandoned once more. October was much longer than those four years after that memorable summer.

## 8

Hai Saeng was back once the second semester of our first junior high year began, and he was gone the next semester break.

I was getting used to his departures and arrivals. When we were first apart, I had to fight this uneasiness in my heart. We had each other's number, and I only ever called him once, in the middle of the night, to get his help on English grammar. I chose the most complicated and lengthy topic of all, which Hai Saeng explained in very simple terms. I placed the mobile phone next to my ears, turned off the microphone on my end, buried my face into my pillow, and let all my yearnings for him rush free in that short moment. 'Is there anything else?' He asked. I gulped, tried to make my voice sound normal, and replied with a question: 'When are you coming back?'

Hai Saeng wasn't annoyed that I was following him around like a goldfish's string of turds. During the last few days of semester break, I spent most, if not all, of it at his place. He raised his brow when I asked to stay over, then burst out laughing.

'I thought you would be scared shitless of ghosts,' he said. 'Sure, it'll be somewhat scary at night though.'

Hai Saeng's house was rumoured to be *haunted* according to the blasphemous gossip that people had conjured from thin air and Hai Saeng's nightly concerto. Hai Saeng had left his mother's piano to collect dust for years, so it was completely out of tune. On that night, I got a ringside seat for his piano session. I sat on the same piano stool as him and kept my eyes glued to his ever-flowing hands, not even paying the slightest attention to how out-of-tune it was.

'How has your semester break been?' I asked.

'Like usual.' He smiled. 'Boring.'

'Is your mom doing okay?'

'Not okay, like usual.'

'Is the rumour true?' I changed the topic and rested my head on his shoulder. 'What people say about the old owner of this house?'

'About the homicide?' Hai Saeng laughed. 'I think it is. This house doesn't have many happy stories to begin with,' he continued while playing the piano in a very nonchalant manner. I noticed him playing something different now. He wasn't playing any song in general—his left hand was playing four chords over and over while his right hand went up and down the octave. Hai Saeng looked at me and said, 'You've never asked why my parents broke up.'

'Why should I?'

'Everyone does.'

'Fine, why did your parents break up?'

Hai Saeng stopped playing the piano and answered, 'Because of me.'

I was somewhat taken aback. 'I don't understand.'

'It's late already,' Hai Saeng cut the conversation short. 'How about we go to bed?'

## 9

We lay talking to each other at two different heights. His bedroom only had one bed, so he took his mattress topper off and laid it on to the floor as my makeshift bed. During our chit-chat, he was lying on his side similarly to a reclining Buddha with his elbow propped up, supporting his head, while he looked down at me. I felt as if I was Hai Saeng's pet dog.

'Will you confess already, Dao Nhue?' he said from up above.

'What?'

'What were you doing when you called me?'

'What was I doing . . . Well, I . . . I was taking notes of what you said!'

'Oh.'

I was the one who asked to stay the night at his place, true, yet it took all my willpower to try falling asleep. Hai Saeng continued talking to me. I closed my eyes in the room that was his—the room that was filled with his belongings, with his scent. We had slept next to each other many times already in the past. Back then, we slept everywhere: beneath that grassy roof, in the garbage dump area once it was freed from people, and on a small fishing boat. We would lie down and count fluffy clouds, watch the sun setting behind the mountain range, float in a calm and shallow river during arid summer, and read rental comic books from an old bookshop the next alley over—reminiscing about our short childhood helped calm my lost heart. Hai Saeng was my friend, and he would remain so, only if I could stop obsessing over him. While the thought was crossing my mind, I felt a soft, cold touch on my back.

It was Hai Saeng's toe.

'Dao Nhue, are you sleeping?'

I felt chills running all over my body. I kept my heart in check and replied, 'Not yet.'

'Turn this way and talk to me, I don't want to talk to your back.' His toe was still prodding at my back. I curled up underneath the blanket.

'I'm sleeping now.'

'So, you really asked to stay over just to sleep?' he teased me. His last few words were uttered in a whisper. 'Are you sure you don't want to come up here?'

I opened my eyes.

'Can I?'

'Uh-huh.'

We lay next to each other on Hai Saeng's small bed. I remained frozen in place for a long while with beads of sweat on my skin even though the weather wasn't that warm. My heart was thumping. A breeze blew through the window curtains. I turned my head around, hoping to ask what he wanted to talk about—it seemed as if he had something he wanted to talk to me about ever since early evening. Once I turned around, I found the familiar face looking my way as well. Then, it happened, like a blink of mirage that had made itself known in the summer long past. Hai Saeng smiled. It was the same smile as that of his eight-year-old self. Moonlight made him look like a spectral illusion. I reached out unknowingly to touch his face. He lifted his hand up to touch my own. Our fingers slowly intertwined.

In the dark shadows, Hai Saeng kissed me. He pressed his lips on to mine, then pulled away, and came back for another soft kiss, teasing, refusing to initiate anything beyond that, waiting for me to lose my control—for which he didn't need to wait long. Just having him tease me innocently like that was already driving me crazy. I kissed him back, hoping to taste the tongue that once adeptly tied a cherry stem, swallowing the breath that once was his.

It happened so swiftly, as if the one whole year where we knew each other only from a wide distance was somehow a joke. I hugged him close to me, waiting for the moment where he would push me off, kick, struggle free, or ask what the hell was wrong with me. He, instead, followed my lead. Hai Saeng flipped himself on top of me, shifted his weight down as I began kissing his neck, then moved his body up once my kisses began trailing downwards. He moaned softly with gritted teeth. His faint voice was much sweeter than I had imagined it would be. On the contrary, all truths that Hai Saeng was moulded out of made my imagination seem more stupid by the minute. Hai Saeng knew, without words, what it was that we were doing. All his movements were only to accommodate me and my touches.

'Did you miss me?' he teased as he let his body fall underneath me. Our positions were flipped around from how we first met. Hai Saeng was lying beneath me, and I was looking down at him. I was the one who stole all the lights from him, fondled him, and trapped him within my arms in a way that I had been yearning for so long.

It all happened so fast. I told Hai Saeng through my actions how I had missed him, and how I had been dealing with that yearning when he was away.

## 10

We spent the night in his narrow bed, skin pressed up against skin, bed sheet and blanket soaked in sweat and other bodily fluids that we hadn't yet learned how to take care of. Come to think about it, we were only fourteen. Was I too hasty? And what was Hai Saeng—he who had a mind much more mature than others of the same age—thinking? Did he know all along that I liked him, or was he just pitying me, seeing me wallow in sadness when he was away? Was it the same as when he did all that his mother asked of him? Could it be that he never paid any mind to how others might treat him? Could it be that what we had meant nothing to him too?

Hai Saeng and I looked at one another. His pitch-black eyes seemed tired, but they were still burning with deeper desires. And there was something else.

I could feel since early evening that Hai Saeng wanted to say something to me, but he couldn't find a chance to. And even if he could, he chose not to say it. This time around, I chose to remain quiet, looked into his eyes, and waited for him to speak. Still, I couldn't remain still for long—I couldn't refrain from kissing him whenever he looked troubled, in hopes of consoling him.

'Dao Nhue.'

He spoke up at last.

'What?'

'Do you see me as someone who's capable of murder?'

'What?'

'*Murder*,' Hai Saeng answered. All my hair stood on end. While uttering that word, he was still pressing his forehead up against my nose, snuggling as if nothing had happened. His damp hair was soaked in our scent.

I gulped, and asked him, while trying my darndest to sound normal, 'Have you done it before?'

'Not yet,' Hai Saeng said. 'It didn't work out—I was in a rush.' I thought back to when he had helped me hide during a hide-and-seek game. He had covered a storm drain with its heavy lid to hide me away from others and had even put a pot of fiddle-leaf fig on top so I couldn't push the lid open on my own. I asked with a chuckle if that was what he meant.

'I was just testing.' Hai Saeng shook his head, a soft smile spreading on his lips. 'I was just testing to see how many hours I had before the body would be found.' He told me that he hadn't planned on actually killing me—he had only wanted to know how long it took for a rescue team to search for a person. 'I planned to go get you by the morning. The amount of oxygen that a person would need to breathe, the level of humidity that a child could possibly weather, or the dehydration that happens from sweating too much—none of those was on my mind.' Regardless, Hai Saeng had been only eight years old back then. That pair of deep ponds glittered with small sparkles when he talked about it. It was as if he was happy. I was glad to know that I was the cause of this joy.

Two fourteen-year-olds lying next to each other and talking about such a morbid topic was perhaps erroneous in all aspects, but I could care less. As long as it was what Hai Saeng wanted.

'Can you tell me about that time you failed?'

Hai Saeng's brow lifted in surprise. He then answered me with a deep, hoarse voice.

'Of course.'

## 11

'Nothing good has ever happened in this house,' Hai Saeng started the story off with a simple sentence. 'I know how you think I'm a child abandoned by his parents, left all alone in a house. Isn't it so, Dao Nhue?'

It was a story that sounded as if it had taken place in a far-away place, when in fact, it had happened at a large house in our village, at the end of a most normal alley.

'It would be better if that's the case—no, I actually pray that it is so.'

Hai Saeng's house once had tenants. It was an old building that had weathered against time and had changed owners often. Many said that its location was inauspicious and that it attracted malicious energy. Hai Saeng's family paid no mind to that. Its beautiful architecture and price lured them to move in. They were just a normal family—a woman and a man who got married too early. They succeeded financially before ever learning about the other's true nature, before the man ever learned that his wife never paid mind to anything save for her fame and glory, and before the woman ever learned that her husband was a paedophile.

'I once believed that I was lucky; I got whatever I wanted, and my parents bought me anything I asked for, so I was too trusting with it all,' Hai Saeng said. 'I only learned that Father had long been trying to do vile things to me when I was already seven.'

Hai Saeng was once a normal kid too. Having learned of this, my body was numbed with anger. He should have been allowed to remain a child, to grow up without realizing that this world is filled with dangers—especially from within one's family.

Hai Saeng continued to recount the story as if it didn't concern him. 'Remember this, Dao Nhue. A human's vital point is right here.' Hai Saeng reached his hand out to rub behind my earlobe, just centimetres away from my temple. 'The skull is thin right here; it can be easily shattered. Even a child can bring a grown-up down with this.'

'How did you learn about this?'

'I observed. I had to observe so many things when I was younger.' At that, he wrapped his arms around me and pulled me on top of him, bending my upper half down to listen to his words. He had me act as his father. I felt as if Hai Saeng was someone else, someone I didn't know. I felt as if my skin was covered with abhorrent worms. Hai Saeng's gaze, too, was so cold that I could hardly bear to look back.

'I hid Father's favourite ashtray underneath his pillow, waiting for him to come closer. I could still smell those rotten breaths. I had to calm down. I had to be patient,' he whispered. 'When he believed that I was frozen in place, having given up, that was when I slowly got out the ashtray and struck it right here.'

He pressed his finger underneath my temple and added pressure to it, a smile spreading on his face.

'I struck and struck, and I made sure that it was with enough force each time I did—if not, I would be the one to die. If I let him gain footing, I was sure that he would suffocate me with a pillow until I was dead. I kept hitting until he rolled over.'

'But he didn't die?' I furrowed my brows.

'No.' Hai Saeng's gaze was blank. 'How could a seven-year-old think through things, Dao Nhue? What a pitiful boy he was.' His mind had already drifted away somewhere else. Then, it seemed as if he remembered something and laughed so loud that I jumped. 'Mother came home and found me in my tattered clothes dragging Father on the floor. She passed out seeing that! What an image that was—a woman that never showed any emotion, passing out in front of me. I should have cherished that short moment just a bit more—if only I knew that Father would wake up in a hospital after Mother's hysterical attempt at finding help. Everyone lost their mind. That was when I headed back to my bed and had a sweet dream for the first time in years.'

It was a mess after that event. His parents couldn't look each other in the eye. His mother was afraid that her name would be tarnished, so she moved back to stay with her family—one that found a strange child like Hai Saeng repulsive. What followed next was a divorce, an attempt at rearing a child based solely on money and void of affection, and a child that grew up distorted. None of Hai Saeng's stories were visible through his smiles apart from the truth that he was utterly good at concealing all the hatred he held against others, and that the said hatred seemed to have already swallowed all those blissful days from his memory of our summer. I softly patted his hand and consoled him as much as I could. Hai Saeng, however, remained quiet for a long while before taking both of my hands to grab around his neck.

'Kill me, please, Dao Nhue,' he said.

'Huh?'

'Kill me now, before I grow up to kill others.'

## 12

The semester break came to an end. We returned to our normal lives as eighth graders, save for how I quit the football team and all other extracurricular activities to spend my time studying with Hai Saeng in the evening. Extra lessons were a good excuse to stay next to him with my mom's approval—actually, she was elated. She was elated to see her academically doomed son finally studying to make it through a famous high school's entrance exam, and the fund for his extra lessons wasn't a problem if the family could cut some expenses (Dad's orchids and tropical fish, for instance).

Hai Saeng stopped going to places with his driver. He had lately been riding on the backseat of my motorbike to go to school, his tutoring school, and even had me drive him home in the evening. He stopped resting his face against my back during his rides, as he now had a personal helmet—a black one, one I personally chose for him.

We had been sticking much closer to each other than before. I cared not for what others said; whenever someone looked at us, it only spurred my desire to hug Hai Saeng's shoulder close to me. Hai Saeng would only spare a glance and smile in silence, not even once conjuring up any excuse to please his EP classmates, not even when they whistled and teased us. He liked seeing me act like his pet dog anyway, and it elated me to see those people flabbergasted when I carried Hai Saeng away from the middle of the hallway. We laughed whenever we thought of those people, as if they were only insignificant backdrops to a story.

On that night, the one when Hai Saeng asked me to kill him, I didn't do it. We let go of each other and went to sleep separately. 'This will help calm us down,' Hai Saeng said as he turned the other way. I went back to the mattress on the floor, closed my eyes, and listened to his steady breathing until dawn. That was the first time I ever had a chance to feel a broken being. Those broken surfaces didn't lessen my desire towards him.

Not in the least.

## 13

On Loy Krathong night, Hai Saeng and I sat on the edge of the bridge that we hadn't visited together for so long. This bridge stretched between our suburb village and a riverside market with the Phetchaburi River, our province's most important river, rushing beneath. This was the place where Hai Saeng and I built our secret hideout six years ago.

Rivers were filled to the brim with water in November, and some years, the water even spilled into floods. Those living in the market area were already used to moving their belongings away from the reach of the flood and reinforcing the floor of their houses with concrete. Some even put up a low brick wall around their front door to keep water out, and they had to hire construction workers to tear the wall down once the flooding season passed. Luckily, Kaeng Krachan Dam had already released some water into irrigation canals earlier that year, so the water level sat right at the brim. The twilight air was filled with young couples sending their Krathongs off on to the river, and their chatter didn't sound too different from twittering birds. A full moon hung high up in the sky, casting its reflection on the river. Krathongs made of banana leaf floated beneath the moonlight, incense sticks and candles glowed amidst dark water, and young children swam about, picking up loose change from the Krathongs.

'There's no privacy at all,' I grumbled.

'Why did you choose to come today, then?' Hai Saeng was enjoying his ice cream sandwich in a bun without a care in the world. There was no Krathong in our hands nor our minds. 'I have been cursed enough already, so why piss off Goddess Ganga by adding more waste to her'—thus said Hai Saeng when I went to pick him up with my motorbike.

'If I didn't, someone would have asked you out instead.'

'Hmm?'

'To float a Krathong together, you know what that means.'

I thought back to those from our school, upperclassmen and students from freshmen year alike. Their hungry gazes, burning with desire to pull Hai Saeng away from me, pierced me with all their tangible annoyance. I had always kept my eyes on Hai Saeng ever since the night we made love. It seemed as if what we did that night had pulled a mysterious trigger underneath Hai Saeng's skin, releasing him from his childish cocoon into a young man in the blink of an eye. His facial features grew handsomely into place, unlike me with my lanky, immature limbs. His darkest, most scariest deep ponds that once held only void now turned into the alluring eyes of a doe. His airy personality, however, took an entirely different turn.

'Why should I act at other's bidding?'

'To make me regret not having asked you beforehand?'

'Dao Nhue, oh Dao Nhue. Who else could be as hopeless as you?' Hai Saeng grinned, his voice swallowed by the noisy chatter. 'Who would like me?'

It was impossible that someone like him wouldn't have realized how popular he was, in spite of all his airy unconcern for others. Well, whatever, it might be all in my head—one thing that had drastically changed was how Hai Saeng had ceased to contain all his evilness to blossom only within his mind. A myriad of depraved topics were spread in front of us whenever we were alone together. Our conversations flowed ever smoothly as we laughed, trampling on all moral decencies. I wanted to prove to him that I could be trusted, so I went with his flow. How could I have known that everything would come together from that night onwards?

'Dao Nhue.'

'Yes, Hai Saeng?'

'Do you remember our grassy hideout?'

'I do.'

'Do you think we could hide a body down there?'

This was an example of our depraved topics. Chills ran up my spine. 'Whose body?' I asked. Hai Saeng had already finished his ice cream and was licking his sticky fingers. 'Anyone's,' he turned to look at me with an innocent pair of eyes, as if the conversation he had instigated just now was a most normal one—as if we were talking about a newly-opened place for good food, or about how he wanted to buy a couple more bins.

'I don't think so,' I answered. 'Not in this season, otherwise the body would float up for all to see—unless you want to be on the news?'

'Wouldn't summer be worse?' He licked a piece of peanut that was stuck to the corner of his mouth. 'It would smell bad after a few days, and there won't be any place to hide.'

'The beginning of the rainy season, maybe?' I leaned in to nibble at his lips, pretending to wipe away what was left of his ice cream, when in fact I was just looking for an excuse to kiss him. 'Our grass shack was buried under water in one night, and the treasures we painstakingly gathered were gone with the water. With an early seasonal storm, people probably wouldn't notice if we weigh the body down with some sandbags, or stones, or . . .'

'Do you think my father would be too big for the shack? We were only around a metre tall back then.'

Hai Saeng turned to look me in the eyes. By then, I realized what he wanted to say.

I looked back at him, shrugged my shoulders, and kept my voice as unwavering as I could.

'I don't want your dad in our secret hideout.'

## 14

As the night went on, more people came. We were still standing right next to the bridge railing. I looked on as pretty Krathongs were whisked back up with landing nets, had their burnt incense sticks and candles replaced with new ones, and then made ready to be sold anew, complete with a steep price. How easy it was for those in the market community to earn their living.

'Dao Nhue, did you swim looking for coins when you were young?'

Hai Saeng shoved his hand into his pocket. It seemed like he had brought something along. I looked at the children that were swimming about and collecting coins from Krathongs down there, most of them rowdy elementary schoolers. I shook my head.

'I couldn't—Mom would be so mad.'

'Your mother cares about jinxes? That you would be stealing from Goddess Ganga?'

'Not that, it's just dangerous. It'd be different swimming in shallow water during the day, right? It's nighttime now, and there are rocks and branches down there. You'd drown if you weren't careful and got caught by those.'

'Where?' Hai Saeng leaned closer to me. My heart fluttered. 'Which area has a lot of branches?'

I pointed to the area directly below us. 'Do you see the top of that branch, where a Krathong is caught? Right there.'

I turned around to see what he was doing. He dug out a burlap pouch, looked at the ten-baht coins in the pouch smugly, then began counting them one by one. I reckoned there were at least thirty or forty of them in the pouch.

'Hey, you guys,' Hai Saeng yelled at the river down below. There was a lamp pole casting its light behind us. The kids, swimming beneath us, only saw Hai Saeng and I as two dark figures, but they could certainly see the light caught at the edges of the coins—the coins that Hai Saeng dumped all at once from the burlap sack into the river.

'Have fun picking them up!'

At that, Hai Saeng smiled a cute smile. The result of his action, however, was nowhere near cute. The river that was once flowing ever so slowly with Krathongs drifting away in lines had turned into a chaotic pond of hungry iridescent sharks within the blink of an eye. With a dozen children that had no mind to yield to one another, all darting towards the coins of undetermined amount, kicking and stomping at each other, the Krathongs that were sent off the shore in the most solemn manner were toppled in their chaotic rush. Some of the children got caught by the branches and nearly drowned, but they somehow managed to swim up to the surface after a short while. 'These children have been living near the river since forever, so they're good at swimming,' I told Hai Saeng. He clicked his tongue in annoyance. What a little devil—I could tell what he had been hoping for.

Some got wounded from clashing with others in the river—hitting their heads, throwing punches at each other, and the like. That was when someone started looking for the cause of the ruckus. *Shit*, I thought. I then grabbed Hai Saeng's wrist and fled from the scene.

'Dao Nhue.'

'What?'

'Do you think they could pick all the coins up?' Hai Saeng asked while running, softly panting.

'Who cares?' I answered with a chuckle. Then we rode my motorbike home.

## 15

'Hai Saeng,' I called him.

'Hmm,' he muttered back, not looking up from his homework.

'Have you noticed that you have been growing up?'

'I'm getting taller by roughly eight centimetres a year.'

'Not that, I meant other parts of your body.'

'Have they?'

'Haven't you noticed?'

Hai Saeng furrowed his brows. *So, he hasn't.* He observed me from the other end of the table, his chin resting on his hand, and concluded, 'You look the same,' with a voice that sounded slightly annoyed. I asked why he was pissed off.

'You look exactly the same, but taller. You were a shorty following behind me not too long ago, so how can I not be pissed off?'

We stood up and compared our heights. I was about twenty-five centimetres taller than Hai Saeng, and he seemed quite annoyed. Although he was skinny and pale as if he had been locked up away in his house, whenever we used to play together outside, others would think that he was the older brother and I the younger; he was the leader and I the follower. He had been the one who decided what we would do and where we would explore on a daily basis, and I was used to being the outsider of every group of friends. With my cowardliness that had barred me from getting along with others and my fear of being left behind, I had agreed with whatever eight-year-old Hai Saeng had said. Such was our relationship back then. I didn't think that I would ever meet anyone else with the exact details as his.

However, something strange occurred near the beginning of winter the year when we were in eighth grade. I met another *Hai Saeng*.

On one certain Wednesday, it was raining hard. The news of a tropical depression from Laos was broadcast on TV. I picked Hai Saeng up from his house with my motorbike at dawn. He had given me a spare key to his house so I could enter the building without disturbing him as he lounged lazily in his bed on the second floor. I, with a raincoat on, parked my motorbike underneath a tree canopy and unlocked the wrought iron gate. Rain was falling, thundering. In the rain, I heard a piano rendition of 'Yad Petch' drifting from the centre of the house. The sound that bounced off the piano's soundboard was crystal clear. Hai Saeng had never played this song before, and I felt that something was off.

I opened the front door and moved my feet, soaked wet, across the parquet floor. I spotted a silhouette sitting up straight on the piano stool. He was a man with a broad forehead, high nose bridge, black eyes, and hair neatly combed up in a slicked-back style. I nearly addressed him 'Hai Saeng', but no, he wasn't Hai Saeng. He was much more grown up and had a hint of timidity embedded within the creases on his face, a pair of brows that were strung up in a line with his focused state, and stubble on his chin.

'So, you're here already, Dao Nhue?'

Hai Saeng greeted me, his voice coming from the staircase in the back. I looked away from what was in front of me and hurriedly turned around to see him. The real Hai Saeng was in his school uniform, looking at the man who was playing the piano with an indifferent gaze.

I lifted a hand up to cover my mouth and whispered, 'Is this your dad?'

What a dumb question that was—Hai Saeng hated his father. If that really was him, Hai Saeng would have had more of a reaction to his presence and wouldn't just glance indifferently at the man. The identity of this man, however, was undecipherable to me. Hai Saeng shrugged and replied curtly, 'Uncle.'

Uncle, or Na, to be precise, means a younger sibling of one's mother. He seemed to be around thirty.

Hai Saeng's uncle continued playing the song until its last note, and only then realized that I was present in the house. His extreme surprise made me regret comparing him to Hai Saeng. *What's this, isn't he just like a rabbit—* something in his demeanour put me in a good mood and had me glancing after him. I raised my hands to greet him with a wai, and he greeted me back. Then he said, 'Nong Nhue, yes? I'm . . .'

'Don't you have to tend to the shop, uncle?' Hai Saeng asked, interrupting him.

'Gosh, I told you already that I don't need to at the moment,' he replied. 'It's temporarily closed for renovation, have you forgotten already? Your mom asked me to look after her son. I heard you dismissed your driver as you pleased, how naughty you are, boy.'

'I can look after myself.'

'Right, right, you can look after yourself—I saw that already—and that's how there's a pile of junk food in your fridge. Still, this house is pretty spacious, so you wouldn't mind having me living here too, no?' he continued, having already forgotten about introducing himself to me, as Hai Saeng intentionally made him forget about it. He drove us to school that morning. Hai Saeng said that we would walk back home in the evening if the rain had ceased, as there was only a two-kilometre distance between the house and the school, so there was no point in picking us up. Hai Saeng's uncle shrugged lazily. 'Whatever,' he said as he pulled his car over for us to get off in front of the school gate.

'What were you looking at?' Hai Saeng jabbed me with his elbow when it was just the two of us.

'I was just thinking . . .' I opened my umbrella and tilted it towards him. 'It was as if I got to see your face in an entirely different light. It was funny.'

'What was Mother thinking, sending him over. How annoying. I wonder how long he's going to stay.'

'You would look like him when you grew up.'

'I guess.'

We reached the English Programme class. I said to him, 'Bye, Hai Saeng, I'll see you in the evening,' but he wasn't listening. He had already floated away in his own thoughts.

## 16

I got to see more of Hai Saeng's uncle. He became Mom's regular at her local bistro. And with his easy-going, chill, and somewhat funny personality, he was quickly accepted into our village community. However, I still hadn't figured out his name by then, so I decided to name him 'Uncle H' for my personal musings.

'Call me Brother! Not Uncle—I can't be that much older than you,' Uncle H said.

'We're at least fifteen years apart, I reckon.'

'Oi, what, how can that be?'

Uncle H made an innocent face and looked around, asking other people in Mom's restaurant if he really was old. The aunties sitting around all laughed, and he followed in their laughter. Such was a personality that you couldn't possibly see from Hai Saeng—he laughed, but not with others. His smiles existed to look down on them, to declare victory when he successfully riled up his surroundings; his was not to socialize.

With the arrival of Uncle H, the neighbourhood was no longer scared of the haunted house at the end of the alley. Whenever he had free time, he would mow the lawn until its thick, green grass was unrecognizable. Coatbuttons and mosses were scraped off the wall, and green lichens on drainage pipes were washed away. The house was much brighter, no longer a man-eating monster. Mom and I unanimously agreed that it was a very beautiful house. At dusk, bright piano tunes playing Thai oldies could be heard from the house, turning our small village into a most romantic one. The drunkard uncle that used to play chess with his neighbouring fortune-teller lady even moved his base to a marble bench at the edge of the garbage dump. They would sometimes shout, requesting their favourite songs, which the sweet Uncle H gladly obliged. The old man's voice singing the lyrics '*How strangely does our world turn, with this fated love that brings two people close . . .*' reached my house. I, lounging around reading a comic book at the moment, jumped.

'I changed the strings and tuned it. Your mother's piano is like new,' Uncle H showed off his work. Hai Saeng shrugged his shoulders nonchalantly—the reason he liked that piano was due to its pitchy, off-tune sound that scared people away and kept them from messing with him. Still, he said nothing in rebuttal; Hai Saeng wasn't too talkative when in the presence of grown-ups.

Uncle H continued to brag to my mom's customers, 'If you like, please come listen at the house. You're most welcome. If anyone has children that want to learn how to play, I can teach. It won't cost much at all.' I massaged my temple when I heard him say that. What would Hai Saeng think if his house turned into a playground for parents to drop their children off? Should this man be doing as he pleased to this extent?

One day, Mom had me deliver food to Uncle H at the house. I took the opportunity to say, 'Hai Saeng doesn't like being around a lot of people. I think you know that already?'

'I do.' Uncle H gave me a gentle smile. 'I know that the two of you are close, and you probably don't like it when someone butts in. But that kid needs to grow up. He'll have to leave this place one day, to enter a university, to have a good future; he can't continue to lock himself in this house, do whatever he wants, and be this rude forever.'

*He'll have to leave this place one day.* This sentence was much more painful than I thought.

'You don't know what happened to him, right, Uncle?'

'Know what?'

*Are you freaking stupid, Dao Nhue. Do you realize what you're saying?*

'Nothing.'

'I didn't put my nose in my sister and her husband's quarrel and their divorce, Nong Nhue. You shouldn't put your nose in grown-up stuff either. To be honest, my sister told me to take care of her son so we can get acquainted.'

'Why do you need to get acquainted with him?'

'If that kid got into a high school in Bangkok, my sister would have him stay with me.'

I heard something *snap*.

My world spun. Memories of the past two years whooshed past me scene after scene: Hai Saeng returning, Hai Saeng departing, Hai Saeng being picked up after school every day, Hai Saeng who lived alone in the haunted house and was negligently taken care of just enough so the society wouldn't slam his guardian, Hai Saeng who was much more mature than children of the same age because he had to look out for things since childhood, Hai Saeng who was shoved around as others pleased.

'So, that's it.' I didn't realize that I was speaking in a lower tone. 'Seems like they're really good at pushing their burdens others' way.'

Uncle H stopped walking; his eyes widened as if he couldn't believe his ears. 'What did you say, Nong Nhue? Did I mishear it?'

'I said,' I continued, trying to adjust my tone of voice, 'parents are really good at pushing their burdens away.'

Uncle H furrowed his brows. 'Hey, listen to me. All parents only want good things for their children, Nong Nhue. You're still so young.'

'Can't Hai Saeng choose anything for himself, then? His mom never stayed around, and his dad's a fucking asshole.'

'Nong Nhue!'

Numbness spread on my cheek, followed by a long silence. It was so quiet that I could hear cicadas screeching. My face was turned to the side, and Uncle H seemed somewhat shocked himself. He had slapped me. His hand was raised in the air, frozen in place. His hand must have felt the pain too. His eyes said sorry. He hadn't wanted to do it. That much I knew.

'I'm sorry.' He was the first one to say something, his voice as weak as a flickering candlelight.

'Don't worry about it.' I handed him the food box and walked away.

I knew it was wrong of me to be unable to contain my emotions. Uncle H shouldn't have had to deal with my anger—he didn't know anything about that household at all. He was just one of those few who wished well for Hai Saeng in his cold and desolate world. I promised myself that I would apologize to him and treat him better. I would talk to him when Hai Saeng completely ignored him. I thought that he ought to be treated fairer, but the truth that Hai Saeng's family and future would take him away from me only troubled my mind to no end.

Nighttime came. I looked at the fluorescent light piercing through the curtain of my window. I sent Hai Saeng a text message.

> Are you taking the exam for T school in Bangkok?

Not even five minutes had passed when a notification sounded. His answer was short and simple.

> Of course.

## 17

Hai Saeng's message had my eyes widening in shock. I threw my phone into the laundry basket, listened to a soft thump, then turned around to hug my pillow and lay still. I tried to calm myself, but I didn't succeed. I was angry. That answer angered me. That 'of course' played on loop in my head. 'Of course.' I tried to analyse the words. 'Of course' had the same meaning as 'Yes, I'm leaving this place, I'm leaving you.' Regardless of who it was that made this decision, his mom or he himself, the result remained the same: that house would be abandoned, he would have a new circle of friends, and I would rot to death in a village forgotten by time.

I looked at the wall. The clock's second hand moved in a smooth tick-tock-tick rhythm. My cheek remained numb, even when the pain was no longer there. Those two-timers who get slapped by their girlfriends when the truth comes out probably felt something similar, no? It was more of a shock than a pain. A slap takes a shorter time to be delivered, and it was filled to the brim with the pain of the perpetrator themselves. I occasionally got into fights. My brows would break and bleed, and my face would be bruised for days, but those punches didn't incur the same guilt in me as what Uncle H had left behind. Different thoughts swarmed me for a long while until my stomach ached. I decided to stop talking to Hai Saeng for the time being. He might feel nothing, but I wasn't ready to face everything just yet.

*Ping.*

A soft notification sounded from the laundry basket. My mobile phone's display screen lit up. I hurriedly scooted over to check it.

Hai Saeng had sent me a message.

> Dao Nhue, why did my uncle slap you?

> You saw that?

I texted him back right away (pray forget the part where I said I would stop talking to him).

> Of course, my heart was thumping.

Gosh, he must be the only one who could say out-of-place stuff without reading the room and not anger me. Actually, no. I was still angry. I was really angry at him, but I didn't know how to deal with the anger—I had never been angry at him before. To be precise, we never fought because I was too scared, and Hai Saeng would replace his anger with indifference; he kept his emotions in check behind a smiley mask. His text message erased all numbness I felt on my cheek from being slapped by Uncle H.

I texted him again.

> I want to see you.

And Hai Seng instantly replied.

> If you do, then look down.

Outside of my window, the floor below, outside of the house fence, underneath the dull light of a lamp post, Hai Saeng was there, waving at me. He wore casual clothes for a day out with a black cap on his head and a small rucksack on his back. He looked down to type another text.

> Bring your clothes and bike key too.

My heart went thrashing against my rib cage when I read his next text.

> We're running away together.

## 18

The motorbike roared into the night at 60 km/h, as per the speed limit.

'Where are we going?' I asked.

'The horizon,' Hai Saeng put up a serious voice, then reached his arms out to hug my waist. He was copying nineties Hong Kong movies. The warmth of his skin slowly seeped through our clothes. I took a deep breath in.

Alas, we didn't make it to *the horizon*. My motorbike, whose main function was to get groceries, wasn't suited for such a rough journey. The province we lived in was a big one, complete with its own city, forests, agricultural fields, and sea—we had to choose one out of the four. Hai Saeng said that he didn't care about our destination, as long as it was out of Uncle H and my mom's grasp. So, we rode through the marketplace and headed for the outskirts of the city where there were abandoned buildings for bird's nest businesses, salt pans, cockle farms, brackish water, and mud beach.

After half an hour on the road, we finally crossed the arch bridge which marked the end of the river. Our surroundings got darker instantly; Bang Tabun subdistrict wasn't much of a tourist destination, so there weren't many streetlights, and the streets were full of stray dogs. Hai Saeng clicked his tongue. I knew that he hated dogs— he wanted to throw something at those noisy four-legged animals, but he didn't have any rocks in his reach.

I parked my bike to get more gas and asked the station attendant in the meanwhile if there were any cheap guesthouses in the area.

'Didn't you make any reservations?' The attendant asked. I shook my head. She pointed into the dark. 'There are homestays along the beach. They are run by the locals—not sure if they'd still be open this late in the night though.'

The motorbike continued its journey into the darkness. It felt as if we were in the middle of a desolate world, which was made up of nothing. Even the tall buildings on the sides of the road were mostly occupied by birds, twittering as if to drive out trespassers. I stopped by small hotels in the area. Closed, closed, and closed—it took my fourth try to find a place with a vacant room to rent. The one tending to the reception was an old lady with a liquor bottle in her arm. 'Where's your parents?' She mumbled as she held her hand out, waiting for my ID card to record into the registry.

ID cards? None. We were fourteen years old—a pair of runaway youths. Having only realized this truth, I felt instant chills. I looked at Hai Saeng. He smiled, took out his wallet, and placed a card on to the table. The old lady swept her eyes carelessly over it and looked at him over her glasses.

'You look younger than this photo.'

'The district's camera was choppy, Granny.'

'Yes, yes, it's like that.' She handed him back the card. 'There's morning alms tomorrow, want me to wake you up?'

'No, thanks. We're just looking for a place to stay during our road trip.'

'But you want breakfast, right?'

'That would be great.'

'That's your room, the cabin right there.'

The old lady handed us a key and pointed towards a fisherman's cabin on the other side of the road. We crossed over and got ourselves a room—it was that simple.

The small cabin, made entirely out of wood, stood on a mud beach. Some ten poles held it in place, albeit not too firmly. Once we opened the door, we were greeted with a small, incomplete world: a window that opened to a vast water surface, poles atop two thin mattresses with a mosquito net attached to them, a ceiling fan, a yellow light bulb, a wash basin and a shower head, and pretty much nothing else. Hai Saeng and I flopped down on to the mattresses, bone-tired. We lay there, staring at each other for a while, and burst out laughing.

'What are you thinking about?' Hai Saeng asked.

'I'm thinking that it's just like our secret hideout—this sorry excuse of a ceiling.'

'It's a bit larger though.'

'With more mosquitoes too.' I let the mosquito net down around us. 'You stole your uncle's card. Did the granny at that counter not look at your birth year?'

'She probably simply let it pass. Economy's bad; any customer's better than none,' Hai Saeng made a half-hearted guess. 'Why did my uncle slap you, though, did you break his heart?'

'It's a long story.'

'Or rather, did you pick a fight with him? Like . . .' he propped himself up in a half-sitting position, leaned in closer with a teasing smile on his face. He softly whispered, 'Hai Saeng and I haven't had any good fucks ever since you came to live here.'

'Hai Saeng!' My face was burning up.

'Tell me, then.'

'You don't need to know.'

'I think I do have the right to know.' He smiled gleefully.
'I have been taking good care of you, never allowing any
wounds to grace your skin, no?' I glanced at his eyes. That
pair of deep, dark ponds were muddy with discontent. Hai
Saeng smiled. 'If my dog barked, the one to scold him should
have been me. Who was that old man, then? How nosy.'

'Do you also feel possessive over me?'

'Why? Not happy?'

'I'm happy.'

I wanted to tell Hai Saeng what exactly took place
that evening, but his words and smile ignited the fuse of
a bomb that I had been bottling up inside. Hai Saeng was
about to ask something else. I didn't allow him to. I grabbed
him, kissed him, and he kissed me with a bored look on
his face—I *knew it'd turn out like this*—the words were
spoken through his side glance. Regardless, he seemed
content that his words had succeeded at riling me up.

Sweat-soaked clothes were thrown outside the
mosquito net. We were still too young, I once thought
to myself, afraid that crossing that threshold with Hai
Saeng would change too many things in my life. After that
night, however, we never hesitated again. I looked at Hai
Saeng, looked at his spread legs as they slowly wrapped
around my waist, at his chest as it raised up and down
with his breaths. He looked like a butterfly as it flaps its
wings; so fragile yet beautiful. It was as if his body was
moulded to make love with someone—with me—and I,
a piece that was made to perfectly fit him. Our bodies
hungered for each other. It was a most innate yearning
rooted deep within our souls. We were no different
from those grown-ups who clung to religions and their

idolatry. I, on the other hand, worshipped Hai Saeng with a prayer that chanted no other words but his name, with kisses tracing his cold skin, with my yearning gaze and words of ceaseless adoration.

Hai Saeng exaggerated about treating me well—*never allowing any wounds to grace your skin*. Judging from the scratch marks he so blatantly left on my back and the kiss marks I left around his joints, one would be hard-pressed to find a couple who left each other as many wounds as we did.

## 19

I woke up at five in the morning. Hai Saeng wasn't next to me. I was so shocked I nearly lost my mind, believing that he must have already left me behind and headed back alone. I looked around the room, saw that his rucksack and clothes were still there, and his shoes too. There was a slip of notebook paper left just outside of the mosquito net. It read, 'Look outside.'

Once I looked out of the window, I saw that the water had risen, reaching almost the top of the poles. Hai Saeng was floating amidst the muddy water, his arms and legs stretched out, relaxing. It was such a good view. I hurriedly put on my football shorts, opened the door to the terrace and jumped into the water after him. Water splashed around me, as cold as ice. The motor of a fishing boat could be heard as it went past us.

'It's cold!' I yelped.

'The sun's not up yet, that's why.' Hai Saeng laughed. 'And this is December, just in case you've already forgotten.'

It had been such a long time since I last swam. I swam around, missing it dearly. 'This sea's not beautiful at all. I should have brought you to another,' I said. Hai Saeng didn't care where we were headed—he only wanted to leave his house. I happened to have a clash with Uncle H, so he found his chance to leave. I reckoned it was a good time to talk to him about that.

'So, what did you do to that old geezer?'

'I stuck my nose where it wasn't supposed to be.'

I closed my eyes. It seemed like cold salt water did help cool my head down. Words poured from my mouth—thoughts I had kept inside, what I thought about Uncle H's actions, *'unwanted goodwill'*, what his mom did, *'controlling your life as she pleased'*. I had never told Hai Saeng about these things. I believed that he didn't want my counselling. Not even the part about me badmouthing his dad. How shameful.

Hai Saeng listened to me and remained quiet. He looked the other way and began to float away.

'I'm sorry. I shouldn't have said any of this.'

I hurriedly paddled after him, thinking, *Damn, I let my mouth run loose.*

'No.' Hai Saeng stopped. Having noticed that I had caught up with him, he leaned back into me. 'Well.' He looked up at me. Fractures within his eyes were crumbling, confused, as he said the last words. 'I'm happy.'

I choked up. My chest warmed up at the same time.

*Hai Saeng was happy?*

'What about you? What do you think?' I tried to speak without letting my tears fall.

'About what?'

'About taking an exam for T school in Bangkok. About us, not being together.'

He listened and went quiet for a long while. It was perhaps due to the anxiety and sadness that welled up, filling my eyes, that Hai Saeng slowly let out his breath.

He said, 'I have been mulling over this too, Dao Nhue.'

'What do you think?'

'I want Uncle to die,' he said. 'Mother, too. All of them should die. As for Father, I must be the one to kill him.'

It was such a cruel sentence that even I couldn't bear to hear it. I imagined Uncle H's grimacing face as he listened to the words 'die' and 'kill' that slipped out of his nephew's mouth, one he was a guardian of.

'Hai Saeng, don't say that.'

Hai Saeng smiled and replied, 'Let me say it. In this world where I can't choose much, I ought to retain the freedom to wish everyone death.'

'I see.' I could only nod. We floated in the water, lounging about, until the sun rose high up in the sky.

## 20

After going up and down the mud beach just below the cabin's terrace for half a day, we lay naked atop our mattress, arms and legs draped atop each other. Our tanned skin stung, most likely from sunburn. Even Hai Saeng with his unusually pale skin was grilled by the sun until his skin turned red. I turned my head to kiss him, our lips dry from salt water. Our eyelids were heavy—we had been lounging about drowsily from dawn.

Hai Saeng asked, 'Have you ever thought about running away from home?'

I shook my head. 'Have you?'

He seemed surprised. Hai Saeng told me that he had always been thinking about running away from home, from when he was much younger up until now, never abandoning the thought. The riverside hideout was one of the factors that supported this idea of his. 'Even though there was no one living in that house except you?' I asked, confused. He nodded. A *symbolic representation of running away*—I coined the term from my own understanding. Then, Hai Saeng asked me to play a game.

'Say, let's think of something. Something you want to do but have never gotten the chance to.'

'Something you can only do when running away from home, you mean?'

'Uh-huh.'

'I have never . . . Hmm . . .' I pondered. I thought back to Bang Tabun trips with my family, family reunions with my cousins with years separating one reunion from another. Older uncles would secure spots in a beachside restaurant, ordering food in such an extravagant manner that Mom was shocked upon seeing the price. Fishermen caught fresh seafood right there at that mud beach. They kept farms of cockles there, and as the fishermen scooped those cockles up with a basket, their mud-covered shells would shimmer underneath sunlight. It was right there that I found my wish. 'I want to have blanched blood cockles, partially raw.'

Hai Saeng furrowed his brows and commented, 'You're weird.'

'My parents won't let me eat raw food, that's why.'

'How much do you want?'

'A lot. Like, a whole lot, with seafood sauce.'

'Well, let's have some then.'

He threw my shirt at my head, and I hurriedly put it on. When I looked up again, I saw Hai Saeng running away with my bike key. We raced to the motorbike. I had never seen Hai Saeng running before, and I only realized just then that he could run quite fast—so fast I nearly couldn't catch up to him. We took a road that ran along the beachside community until we reached a restaurant. The afternoon scenery was much friendlier than that of the nighttime, but much lonelier than it ought to be regardless. We chose an air-conditioned restaurant befitting our mission, then I ordered blanched cockles, and nearly choked on joy when I said to the server, 'A twenty-second blanching would do.'

The server jotted down our order. We ordered a couple more side dishes and soft drinks. Blanched blood cockles were the first dish to be served. I dug the flesh out of its shells using my bare hands, dunked it in the accompanied sauce, and devoured it delightfully. The taste was unlike anything I had ever eaten before—soft, springy, and juicy with blood. When I sucked it into my mouth, there was a loud slurping noise; it was the first time I had seafood with anyone else outside of my family, and I had completely forgotten about the dining table etiquettes that my mom had long been hammering into my head.

'Your mouth is soaked with blood, just like a wild animal,' Hai Saeng commented. 'I hope we won't get diarrhoea, look at how raw it is.'

We began eating at a quick pace. Once we were almost full and our speed dropped, we continued to slowly nibble on what was left as we sat in that luxurious air-conditioned room for the rest of the afternoon. Hai Saeng ordered a bowl of ice cream. He never made it plain if he had any favourite food, and when I had first gotten to know him, I almost believed that he didn't need to eat at all. Ice cream, however, was the only thing that he couldn't live without.

'Revenge is a dish best served cold,' he said while waving his ice cream spoon around in the air.

'You took that sentence out of some soap opera, right?'

'I really mean what I said.' Hai Saeng smiled. 'One day, Dao Nhue, I'll eat a mountain of lime sorbet. I don't care how long. I will wait.'

'But you can have that today too.'

He shook his head and only said, 'Not yet.'

'Hai Saeng?'

'Uh-huh?'

'It's your turn. Something you want to try but never got a chance to.'

'Hmm . . .' he hummed in his throat lazily. Both of us were lounging on our chairs, waiting for the food to be digested, too full to move. 'Let's do that tonight.'

Hai Saeng leaned his head on to my shoulder. His eyelashes tickled me.

**21**

His wish sounded very much befitting him.

'I want to try smoking.' Hai Saeng reached into his rucksack and dug out a pack of cigarettes and a lighter. He had prepared them before the trip, including a small crystal glass ashtray.

'This—don't tell me that . . .' My heart dropped.

'I always have it with me. A good-luck charm is what it is.'

Hai Saeng beamed and tossed the ashtray playfully in the air. It was the same ashtray he had used to strike his dad's temple until the man was unconscious, then dragged him along the floor. He had been only seven years old. 'My father's favourite ashtray—I brought it to school too, you know? When I was in the seventh grade, I thought that it'd be great if someone decided to mess with me, so I could give it a try. But ever since you started following me around, no one tried to lay a finger on me. How unfortunate.'

*How unfortunate*, is it—it was most fortunate, actually. I couldn't imagine him fighting with others in school with an ashtray. If things escalated and he was called into the principal's office, could he claim that it was done in self-defence? Who would use an ashtray that they *accidentally* carried around to defend themselves?

'Have you ever smoked this?' Hai Saeng asked.

I shook my head. 'You?'

He shook his head too. We both wondered what was special about this rolled tobacco. Why was it so desirable, why was it required of stereotypical gangsters to have one hanging at the corner of their mouth, and why did the grown-ups make it seem as if it was so hard to quit?

Hai Saeng held the cigarette between his teeth and threw me the lighter. 'Be my accomplice.' He smiled flirtatiously, eyes half-lidded. It was such an alluring smile that my insides were all jumbled. I hovered my hand around the lighter and lit the cigarette. He closed his eyes, imitating those gang leaders from Hong Kong movies, then drew a deep breath in and blew the smoke to the side.

'How is it?' I was excited.

'Yuck.' Hai Saeng grimaced.

'Is it that bad?'

'Give it a try.'

He handed me the cigarette. I wasn't sure if I really wanted to try it, but I took it regardless. I gave it an awkward try, not knowing how to breathe in, and breathed through my nose and mouth at the same time. The result was me coughing to death, followed by dizziness and more rough coughs.

'It feels like my inside's burning!' I was about to snuff the cigarette out.

'You're exaggerating. Give it to me—what a waste.'

'I thought you didn't like it.'

'Not in the least, but I have to do it. It's a mission.' Hai Saeng laughed and took the cigarette from my hand to continue smoking. After a few more practice puffs, he looked like a professional smoker already. A veil of white smoke hung in the air, draping down close to the surface of the mud beach. We sat on the terrace, our backs leaned into the wall of the cabin, and our legs dipped into the water. 'It isn't as bad when you're used to it. Now, open your mouth and close your eyes, Dao Nhue.'

'What are you doing?'

'I'm ordering you.'

I could never go against his command. Deep down, I knew that he was going to play tricks with me whenever he said that. It was a battle between *not wanting* and *eagerly waiting*. It was a punishment and a reward that I alone would ever be bestowed. Hai Saeng didn't make me wait long. He leaned his face in to feed me hot cigarette smoke, directly from his mouth. It was pure toxic fumes, freed of anything healthy. My face was hot, and my eyes were irritated. I wanted to cough, but I had to hold it in. I wrapped my arms around his waist and looked into that gleeful pair of devilish eyes, and instead of chiding him or telling him to never do that again, we kissed for the longest time.

As for the poor cigarette, Hai Saeng already snuffed it out before it was even halfway burnt. He put the ashtray back into his rucksack and gave the rest of the pack away to fishermen in the vicinity of that homestay business.

## 22

I couldn't sleep that night. Our mobile phones had been dead since yesterday. It was as if we had planned to not pack any charging cables, and even if we had, I would probably be annoyed by all the incoming calls from Mom and end up turning it off. I didn't know what time it was. We had no clocks and could only look at the moonlight through the blue mosquito net—sea mosquitoes are too nasty, and sane people shouldn't dare challenge them by stargazing on the terrace in the middle of the night. I turned around to look at my companion. Hai Saeng was sleeping next to me, fatigue visible on his face. Us running away had him working out much more than he was used to, which was a good thing; he was much happier and outspoken compared to when we were with the grown-ups.

Be it from overeating or half-cooked blood cockles, I lay on the mattress with an upset stomach and its thundering and rumbling. Hai Saeng flipped on to his side, facing the other way. I muttered a sorry, which he must not have heard. I tried to think about uplifting topics to lull myself to sleep—what to do tomorrow, where to go next when I was bored with this place, which sea had the best scenery, would Hai Saeng enjoy the mountainscape, and which job I could do if I stopped studying. Hai Saeng and I would stay together and never be apart. Hai Saeng wouldn't have to leave for Bangkok alone. But if that was the case, how would we live? Would Mom search for me—would she cry? And would Uncle H blame it all on himself?

I curled up on the stiff mattress and dirty pillow. The wooden cabin in which the two of us lay pressed up against one another had turned into a most loathsome place, complete with the pitchy screeching of the sea breeze as it seeped through rotten walls, a tattered roof above our heads, a shoddy electric fan, and creaky support poles above the seawater. I thought back to my cramped room back at home. My family was in no way rich, but we had a well-secured house where we didn't have to worry about being swarmed by mosquitoes the whole night, and there was a sturdy lock keeping our house safe from burglars. Hai Saeng was no different. Truth be told, his haunted house had turned into a rather nice one after Uncle H was done with his scrubbing—it was bright, lively, and no longer an abode of demons. What were we doing here? Why were we running away? Was life not much more carefree with someone making sure that your compulsory education was secured without having to struggle for it?

At last, I came to understand the reason why birds raised in captivity always flew back to their cages, their incarceration. It was the emptiness that settled in your stomach, the insecurity, the doubt you cast on your own pair of wings—many restrictions of youth held us back. That was when fear grasped my heart.

'Hai Saeng,' I called.

'Uh-huh,' he answered.

'Are you not sleeping?'

'I'm awake.'

I shakily whispered, as if I was afraid of divine retribution, 'Hai Saeng, should we go home?'

'Let's do it,' he answered as simply as that. I didn't expect such an answer—it was so simple that I was taken aback. Hai Saeng continued, asking, 'Why, were you afraid that I'd be angry?'

'Yes.'

'If we wait until morning, we'll wake up on a Sunday, Dao Nhue.' Hai Saeng looked at the spinning ceiling fan.

'I asked you to leave on Friday evening, so you didn't skip school, didn't miss a single thing.'

I didn't understand it just yet. Hai Saeng turned around to look at me and laughed.

'I knew that we weren't going to make it far with our running away—I just wanted to make those people lose their heads. Besides . . .' He stuck out his tongue and revealed an empty wallet. 'I paid for the room this evening, so there's no cash left.'

'But I have some with me!' I objected, even though I was the one to propose the idea of going back. It was apparent that I was more afraid of him being disappointed in me than anything else.

'I won't live in poverty with you, just so you know; I prefer an easy lifestyle.' Hai Saeng sat up, his eyes deadly serious. 'You're pretty attached to your mother too, no? I know that you left her a note on the dining table just before you left, telling her, "*I'll be going on a trip.*"'

'I didn't!'

We laughed and looked into each other's eyes in the dark. 'Let's swim?' I asked. He nodded. We took off our clothes and jumped down from the terrace. The water was much colder than yesterday. Hai Saeng was floating on the water surface right next to me, seemingly swarmed with things to say. Still, he wasn't one that liked to tell personal stories. Judging from years of knowing him, I knew about him the most, but it was still not much compared to how I always blabbered on about myself.

'Hai Saeng.'

'Uh-huh.'

'We should have gone on trips much sooner, don't you think?'

Hai Saeng didn't say anything. Judging from his face, I believed that he agreed with me.

'Some other time—no, maybe just once in a while—can we do this again? Let's go somewhere you like, so we can try more things that are new to us. We can do bad things—I'll help you with it. You can hate the adults, 'cause I'll always be on your side. When we finish junior high, you can go to Bangkok; I won't hold your back, not until you're free.'

Hai Saeng furrowed his brows in confusion. I smiled, finally understanding what I had wanted to say to him. 'I just want you to relax more. I don't want to see you suffer.'

'Sure,' Hai Saeng interjected, unable to bear any more of the cheesiness in my speech. It was quite a long moment before he smiled. A smile that wasn't looking down on the whole world. 'Let's go on a trip together again,' he said, and then swam the other way.

The new day's sun rose up above the water surface. Two children were lying on the cabin terrace, waiting to dry up. We caught whiffs of saltiness from each other's hair. And once we were wide awake, our short vacation came to an end.

## 23

Small punishments aside, my mom was quite level-headed, not having already reported to the police that her son had gone missing without a word for two days.

'Knowing that you disappeared along with Saeng dear, I thought that it was probably nothing to worry about—Saeng is always a good kid, no?' my mom said with the sweetest voice.

'I'm not that good of a kid, Auntie,' Hai Saeng answered along with his trademark smile.

'So,' I hopelessly interjected, 'why am I the only one who has to wash dishes as a punishment?'

'Can you stop whining, Nhue? You brought your friend to face hardships, see? Your friend's arms are covered with mosquito bites. Saeng dear, poor you! Did Nhue have you camp out on bare dirt so your skin is all red? Nhue, you good-for-nothing son, you made your friend's family all worried, and no one could even reach you. Saeng's uncle cried so hard my restaurant turned into a counselling centre, and that fortune-teller hag and the chess geezer had to chime in to make things worse. My work multiplied, so I set these dishes aside for you to wash. Is that not a good enough reason?!'

Mom used her threatening ogre voice when the words were directed at her son, then the next minute it was all 'Saeng dear' in a coddling voice, reminding me of how millionaires talked to their pet cat. She even bought him an ice cream—her own son was perhaps not as loved as him now. I looked at him, asking for help. '*You were the one who asked me to run away!*' I gestured with my head at the mountain of dishes. Hai Saeng shrugged. He pointed at the mark on his neck—one Mom reckoned was a *mosquito bite*—and grinned in reply. Chills ran up my spines. That wasn't a mosquito bite.

'Don't tell Mom,' I whispered. Hai Saeng narrowed his eyes and raised his index finger up, signalling me to remain quiet.

'Focus on scrubbing those dishes.'

What Mom said about Uncle H was in no way an exaggeration—Hai Saeng's blood-related uncle was crying rivers from Saturday morning until Sunday. He didn't sleep, the whole house was shut close, his eyes were sunken, and his beard was left unshaven. When he saw us standing in front of the house, he ran outside to pull us into a hug. Uncle H was blaming no one but himself. He believed that Hai Saeng ran away because he did wrong by me. A huge drop of tear stained Hai Saeng's shirt. Hai Saeng glanced at me in annoyance and pushed his uncle away. As for me, I had already decided to be nicer to Uncle H.

I hugged him back and said to him, 'It's okay, really. About that day, I was in the wrong too.'

Uncle H half pleaded, half forced Hai Saeng to make a pinky promise to never run away at night again. 'Travelling on a motorbike at night is really dangerous, you know? What if you were robbed? What if you were killed? People these days are horrible, and you two are still so young! What would I do if your mom knew that I'm shitty at taking care of my own nephew.'

'Nothing,' Hai Saeng answered. 'That woman isn't going to care whether I live or die, here or anywhere else.'

'Don't talk like that. Your mom really cares about you.'

Hai Saeng rolled his eyes and entered the house. He didn't hate his uncle—he was only indifferent to him. As for me, I knew full well that the one who cared about

Hai Saeng wasn't his mom, but rather Uncle H ever since the beginning. Uncle H might as well have been the one who had offered to take care of Hai Saeng at this provincial house. Uncle H, however, never deemed himself a worthy enough piece to interfere in the family affair, so he never dared using himself as a bargaining piece. However, this truth warmed my heart. There was someone else who cared about Hai Saeng.

So, from that day onward, I was more open with Uncle H. Being open with someone started with not lying, so I decided to tell him frankly, 'Hai Saeng and I are dating. We're very deeply connected to each other.'

I had no idea why Uncle H fainted as soon as he heard that. Perhaps he hadn't had much to eat—I thought as I walked around Uncle H and made my way upstairs to continue reading comic books in Hai Saeng's room.

## 24

'Tell me everything, Nong Nhue!'

'Tell you about what, Uncle?'

'About you and my nephew!'

'I told you already that we are dating.'

The whole school aside, what with them most likely having already been aware of my relationship with Hai Saeng, Uncle H was the first adult that I revealed this to. I had no intention to tell my parents, and it was not due to embarrassment but because of how both of them (especially Mom) were such loudmouths. If Mom knew something, the whole world would also know. I didn't feel like being the subject of conversation of madame fortune-teller and chess uncle just yet. I told Hai Saeng, 'Your uncle knows about us already,' to which Hai Saeng only shrugged. 'Good. We can do things more openly then.' He smiled and intentionally kissed me when we walked past Uncle H, rendering him a sorry mess on the ground, foaming at the corner of his mouth, muttering, '*How scandalous, I can't believe this is the kid I once knew.*'

To acclimatize Uncle H to my presence, I often asked Mom to sleep over at Hai Saeng's house, the reason being to study. Mom even dreamt big time that I would take the T school exam with Hai Saeng, to which I made no objection. It wouldn't hurt to give this entrance exam a try, better yet, Mom would feel like I'm doing something productive. But whenever it was just Hai Saeng and me in a room filled with his scent, I could never focus. Many nights were spent shifting our bodies against each other until we fell asleep, and many nights resulted in nothing more than caresses and Hai Saeng's sudden moment of bizarre clarity.

'If we placed a dead body on a train track, and had its head rest directly on the steel rail, do you reckon the police would be able to identify the body?' he asked while I was taking his socks off.

'They can even identify chopped up bodies nowadays,' I replied. 'They search from the DNA, personal articles the deceased had on them, hair, loose threads, dirt on the soles of their shoes—no one's identifying bodies from the face alone any more.'

'Is that so?' Hai Saeng propped himself up and rested his chin on his elbow, looking down. 'Sorry, did I kill the mood?'

'No worries.'

'Let's go outside.'

And I would follow him. I would ride my motorbike out in the middle of the night just so, to sit atop a bridge railing with our legs dangling in the air, to watch lights from the two communities flanking the market blinking out one by one—to watch our small town falling asleep. We picked a pomegranate from its tree just right in front of a sawmill, gave it a good twist and took a half each to enjoy its juicy arils. We climbed atop the fence of an old Christian church opposite a private school in the old town area to enter its cemetery and played hide-and-seek for almost an hour, then looked for a secluded spot to sit once we were tired. Hai Saeng gently traced his finger across each name on the headstones and read the name out. 'Boonma Sae-peng,' he read. It was my task to guess what kind of life the owner of that name led.

'A Thai woman, married to a Chinese merchant that hailed from overseas to settle down in the market. Her family objected because they didn't like the Chinese, but they led a loving life nonetheless.'

'How did she die?'

'Of old age, surrounded by her children and grandchildren, twenty-two of them in total.'

'What, hedonism much?' Hai Saeng sighed, bored. He much preferred a tragedy.

On some nights, we would ride on until we reached Saphan Dam, the black bridge, a viaduct that stretched atop a river—a famous place for taking photos. We lay down lengthwise with our heads joining in the centre.

'The first to get up loses,' Hai Saeng declared.

'What does the winner get, and what's the punishment for the loser?'

'The loser must do the reading diary for the winner through this whole upcoming semester.'

'Bring it on, then.'

We lay there for nearly an hour. Feeling the need to take a leak, I started talking to distract myself.

'Hai Saeng.'

He muttered, 'Uh-huh,' in his throat.

'Your uncle, how should I say this—he's much more sensitive than I imagined. Not in a bad way, mind you. He's a good person, but when it comes to family matters, he seems intent on keeping everyone together.'

'Are we going to talk about my uncle, Dao Nhue?' Hai Saeng sounded drowsy. 'He's sick.'

'What's his illness?'

'Something grown-ups have. I don't understand much either,' he pondered. 'Depression. I heard he wasn't like this before; he had his rowdy, rebellious phase too. I once saw a photo of him with long hair and a bandana, riding a big bike.'

'I can't even imagine.'

'Eaten away by time,' Hai Saeng said. 'Have you ever heard this quote, Dao Nhue? "*When childhood dies, its corpses are called adults and they enter society, one of the politer names of hell.*"'

'Never heard it. Sounds weird.'

'The one who said this was Brian Aldiss, an English writer. I believe what he meant is that children have different ways to protect themselves mentally. Children make up for what they lack by creating their own beautiful worlds. Once they grow up, it'll be hammered into them that such worlds don't exist, and they'll end up turning into pitiful adults. As for me, I don't think being abandoned is that much of a problem—I'll have a lot of free time for myself that way—but my uncle thinks that abandoning children on their own is a very serious issue.'

It sounded awful indeed—being shaped by time against one's wishes.

'I don't want to grow up,' I said.

'Should we die together, then?'

'You're out of your mind.'

I saw flickering lights from one end of the bridge. The railway crossing gate that barricaded the road from the bridge was being lowered slowly, signalling an incoming train.

'Hai Saeng,' I muttered, as quiet as a whisper. Hai Saeng didn't answer. I believed that he really had fallen asleep. The track began to shake, a *chuff-chuff* noise rumbled through wooden planks and nails. Chills ran up my spine. A train was incoming, heading straight for where Hai Saeng was lying. He would be first to meet the wheels, then it would be my turn. There'd be two dead bodies left on the track by tomorrow morning. We'd make it to the front page. Then we'd turn into an urban legend.

I raised my voice. 'Hai Saeng, let's go!'

'You get up first,' Hai Saeng said nonchalantly, adamant about winning and losing at the most inappropriate time.

'Okay, I'm up now, now you get up too.' I sprang up and dragged Hai Saeng away from the track with all my might. The train was so close I could hear its thunderous roar. Hai Saeng lazily stretched and said, 'You lose, Dao Nhue.'

'Who cares?!'

'Hahahaha!'

His laugh was a tell-tale sign that he was once again the Hai Saeng that looked down on the whole world. We rolled, tumbling into a nearby bush to evade the train. A small bird that was nesting in the bush chirped in protest. Small gravel got into my shirt, leaving me itchy all over. Then, we felt a quick pull of mass—the train had just passed by. We survived. I was relieved. We then headed home, a home in which Uncle H was pacing around anxiously, having realized that we went outside at night. He was angry. He would often lecture us with a mumbling, annoyed voice like a honey bear with its mouth full of bees. However, he would make us a late-night meal after—omelette with veal sausages, or perhaps Teochew fish porridge. He never let us go hungry, no matter how terrible we were to him.

Then we would escape again. Our first time running away paved the way for us—for our new selves who no longer feared the night or the adults—and knowing that there was a home waiting for us, we were less anxious about the future.

As for this matter, I didn't know what Hai Saeng thought of it. No one knew what sort of mysterious maze was stretching within the boundary of Hai Saeng's mind.

## 25

Summer break turned into the time of the year that I hated the most. Hai Saeng left to attend a tutoring school in Bangkok. He left to stay with his mom. As for me, I had to find something befitting a student that would take a high school entrance exam next year to do. Hai Saeng sent me a workbook specifically for the high school exam through the postal service. '*Finish this whole pile so you don't get deranged. I'll grade it once I'm back*'—was the note attached in his own handwriting. I beamed and was happy the whole day, unaware of the hell that awaited me. The level of difficulty of those mock exams were beyond what I had ever seen before.

Maths wasn't too bad, science was skipped, and social studies was hard, but I could read some books. The problem, however, was English—the mortal enemy that I imagined I would never triumph over in this lifetime. '*Read the paragraph and answer the following questions*'—what a hell of a paragraph! I stared at the paragraph written in an unknown language like a mongoose staring at a cobra, thinking, *Damn, if I can't even answer one question, he would certainly chew my ears out when he comes back.* He had spent two years tutoring me, and I couldn't even solve a single problem? When I planned to cheat and check the answer key, I found that I had underestimated Hai Saeng. My beloved gremlin had already blacked out the whole page with a permanent marker.

'*No cheating.*' A post-it note was attached to the last page of the workbook. I could imagine Hai Saeng's voice as he said these words without even trying. Almond-shaped dark eyes with each end pointing up, the corners of his mouth that perked up as if to mock the listener, the pale skin touched by the setting sun, loose threads of hair around his ears that were caught in the wind. He lifted a book up to cover his face as he yawned, his legs stretching out in a half-sitting posture as he lounged on a bench.

Oh dear, how could I focus now?

I killed time by exercising just as Uncle H would always suggest. 'Can't you two try to have fun doing things that normal teenagers do?! Playing football, badminton, basketball, swimming in a pool—anything but climbing a cemetery fence and laying on a train track. I'm about to go insane.' Uncle H was too much of a worrywart. I was stubborn, and Hai Saeng wasn't much into trying to *have fun doing things that normal teenagers do*, so we never played sports together. Now that both of them were temporarily away, I could finally pursue normal avenues as per Uncle's wish. And since April's hellfire temperature wasn't suitable for outdoor sports, I decided to go swim at an elementary school's swimming pool every two or three days, all the while cramming in a 287-square-metre space with small children. Sometimes, when I saw them running around the pool and playing tag with all their might, I would see Hai Saeng and I in their place—two figures underneath the shade of a tree, walking in mud barefoot, the river reaching up halfway to our knees, eating pomegranate and lime ice cream that was so sour, we squinted our eyes.

*Without you, this town isn't ours any more.*

I sighed and floated atop the water, looking at fat summer clouds that would soon turn into rain clouds.

Without Hai Saeng, this small town was depressingly boring, and I should get used to it. We still had another year together until Hai Saeng would get into T high school in Bangkok (he certainly would, there never was a doubt in my heart). I would take the exam with him, and once the result was announced, we would laugh at my rock-bottom result together before we headed our separate ways. I would stay here, pursue a vocational degree, and look for new friends or something along that line.

As for Hai Saeng, I didn't know what his dream was. Perhaps Bangkok would suit him better—there would be more things to do over there.

Say, what kind of place was Bangkok exactly, and what could you actually do there?

I laughed at myself. How narrow was my vision.

## 26

I hadn't gotten many messages from Hai Saeng; he preferred talking in person. If we were talking while looking at one another or at the same thing, our conversation would flow effortlessly, especially when the topic didn't concern us. We enjoyed talking about other people, enjoyed making stories up, and enjoyed lying. Hai Saeng was the master of lying. His hands never quivered, his lips were always smiling, and he never once blinked rapidly, letting off a goofy air like I did. I was connected to him through our shared experience; once we were apart, there was not much to talk about. To put it frankly, I hated this long-distance relationship.

As summer break neared its end, I only became more agitated—I was just like a sailor that endured his labour work on a ship and leapt into the water as soon as he saw the coast, swimming towards it with a heart yearning for land. Around the end of April where everything was dull, I texted Hai Saeng.

> How are things over there?

He replied, curt and cold.

> The same as always

It was a predictable reply. I heaved out a sigh, feeling the urge to throw the phone away into the laundry basket once more—only if the next message didn't pop up.

> I've a family dinner tonight.
> Father will be there too.

*Father.*

That message sent chills up my spines. Anger ran through my nerves. I had never met Hai Saeng's dad before, but I had already learned to hate this man—a criminal under the guise of a parent, the man who had turned Hai Saeng into a child with emotional turbulence and an ever-pessimistic point of view. I wanted to ride my motorbike to Bangkok right away; I would bring Hai Saeng away from whatever he had to face, just like when we ran away from home. I, however, didn't know anything about Bangkok. I didn't know anything about the outside world. Where would we run off to? What would we do after that? I looked down at my hands—a pair of hands belonging to a fourteen-year-old boy going on fifteen—and while they were strong, they lacked the power to fight back in the world of adults.

> Will you be all right?

> Will I be all right with killing him alone? I don't think so. Mother and Uncle will be there too, and there'll be lots of people where we are meeting. Too bad, but that'll have to be the next time.

I had to resist the urge to strangle myself.

> Stop joking! You know what I meant.

> I know, LOL.

Hai Saeng had once told me about his family dinners. They were a strange ritual that would be occasionally held while Hai Saeng stayed in Bangkok. A ritual—it might be a bit cruel to refer to it this way. Actually, a family is supposed to be a group of people that gather around for dinner without any reservations between them, but the awkwardness in Hai Saeng's family—estranged parents and a son, each donning a mask painted with a smile, having a French multi-course meal at a rooftop bar on the fiftieth floor of a luxury hotel with an unknowing Uncle H sitting between them—was far beyond my comprehension.

> I'm worried about you.

I sent him another text message, each word pulled from my heart.

It was quite a long while until he replied.

It's all right, Dao Nhue, I'm used to it already.

Late at night, Hai Saeng sent me a photo of the food he had on the rooftop of that hotel: clear beef bone broth soup, giant scallops with butter sauce, stuffed quail served with sunroot purée, and ice cream with raspberries. Every single dish was glistening from the light that reflected off the crystal glass surface. I had only seen such dishes in western movies and never once dreamt that they would be real—the idea of having just a taste was out of the question.

Looks yummy!!!

I sent him a message with emoticons to convey how envious I was.

The ice cream was good.

Hai Saeng replied, seemingly nonchalant.

and the rest were as always.

He didn't give me further details on what exactly happened at the dining table between the four of them. Our conversation concluded at that.

## 27

That night, I dreamt that I hopped on a van to visit Hai Saeng in Bangkok, waiting for him in front of a hotel whose name I didn't know, only to jolt awake and fall back asleep, dreaming the same dream over and over the whole night. My unconscious mind was punishing my cowardly self by having me look at what should have happened, what I had wanted to do but didn't. Fortunately, nothing happened. I came downstairs late in the morning as the walking dead to eat, then helped Mom clean the house, do laundry, and wash the dishes.

'You must be lonely without your buddy,' Mom said.

'He'll be back soon,' I told her.

'I'm glad you have a good friend like dear Saeng—he even sent you books. How's your study coming along, by the way? Don't push yourself too hard, or I might feel like calling an exorcist.'

'Ooohh.' I yawned. Mom thought that I stayed up late to read—it was written plain on her face, with the corners of her lips almost reaching her ears. I didn't want to shatter her daydream, and seeing my down-to-earth mom reminded me of last night, of a queer meal of a weird family. There was something that I had long been thinking about but had never gotten anyone's opinion on it. I said, 'Mom, can I ask you something?'

'Shoot.'

'Say, if . . . if someone close to us hurt me when I was younger.'

Her expression changed right at that instant. 'Who? Who hurt you?!'

'Please, Mom! This is why I've never asked for your opinion. That's not it—listen to me first. It's not about me, I mean, if it were you, if someone in your family, someone you trusted, took advantage of you using your confidence in them.'

'Oh,' Mom calmed down and made a pondering gesture. 'Like, if a cousin borrowed my money?'

'Not that.'

'Letting a burglar into the house behind my back?'

I clutched my head. 'You only think about money, don't you? Well, let's say that's the case. If one of our cousins let a burglar into our house, would you mind living in the same world as that person?'

'I'll cane them until their back breaks.'

'After that, then? After you caned them?' I looked at Mom expectantly. 'If you had to see them still, had to dine with someone who allowed a burglar into our house, if you couldn't put that person through justice, if everyone said that you had to get along because they're a family member—what would you do?'

My voice was tinted with anger, even when the matter didn't concern me.

'I might just let it be.'

'What?' That was in no way a satisfactory answer. 'Just so?'

'What could we possibly do, Dao Nhue? Buddha said that we should forgive our enemies—our anger will only eat away at us. Those who did us wrong would have already forgotten about what they did, so why should we hold on to the grudge, dear? When you grow up, you'll understand what I said, Nhue.'

'What if . . .' I wasn't going to give up. 'What if it was an unforgivable kind of act?'

Mom looked at me for a long time, then sighed with a small smile on her face. I only noticed just then how much older my mom had gotten during these past few years. The wrinkles on her face loosened, that pair of hardened eyes were coloured with kindness that she reserved for her son alone. Mom knew that I was confused, but didn't know the cause of it.

'No one knows, Nhue,' Mom said softly. 'No one knows what you ought to do, not until you have to face that problem yourself.'

## 28

Hai Saeng came back with the first breeze of rain.

'I have been tutoring you for two years, Dao Nhue, two whole years.'

And a raging storm.

'What do you mean by not being able to solve even a single problem, huh?'

The summer break would be over in a few days. Hai Saeng and I, trapped inside due to the rain, sat looking at each other in a room on the second floor as my exercise sheets were being graded. As for Uncle H, he was running back and forth, taking care of the garden with the overgrown weeds that sprung up while they were away. When he saw my face, he ran up to me and hugged me, having missed me sorely (I didn't understand why he would miss a brat that had been messing up his life to that extent). Uncle H said, 'Why, Nong Nhue, what have you been doing? Your skin had gotten so much darker.

Oh, dear.' And when I replied, 'Swimming in the pool,' he seemed glad to the point that tears welled up in his eyes—this kid had finally decided to partake in normal activities of normal teenagers.

After enduring Hai Saeng's cold gaze for half an hour straight, he finished grading. The result was as expected: maths was all right, social studies and Thai barely passed, and English was best left unmentioned. Hai Saeng stared at me, his gaze intent.

'You are just . . .' He narrowed his eyes.

'I know,' I whispered, dejected like a scolded dog.

'Abysmal,' Hai Saeng concluded in one word, his demeaning tone sounded as if he was holding something in, only to burst out laughing mere seconds later. It seemed as if his earlier annoyance was only an act. 'I can't believe it! I really can't—are you really so bad at this, Dao Nhue? You . . .' He laughed until I began to laugh too. We rubbed each other's head, yanked at one another's clothes until we lost our balance and rolled down on to the rug floor, laughing breathlessly. I could feel blood pumping in my ears, turning them red. My heart was beating fast, the world was lively once more, and I came to learn how much I missed Hai Saeng's laughter.

'I wish you were here during the summer break,' I said.

'Next year,' Hai Saeng told me. He was lying on his back, looking at the ceiling like he always did. 'Summer next year, okay?'

The exam would take place in the beginning of March, then, whatever the result may be, we would be free the rest of the summer. I dreamt of summer with Hai Saeng, summer with the sun glistening atop the river surface just like when we were eight, but we would be much more free, we would cover much more distance—we no longer had anything to fear. I would ask him to ride a train with no certain destination, stop by a waterfall somewhere, stargaze atop a mountain with the sound of the rushing brook through the whole night, and eat a mountain of lime sorbet. We might visit Bangkok, try some cuisine so expensive that we would head home broke, watch a new movie in the theatre, visit a museum, buy some souvenirs from an art gallery, and maybe try a cup of black coffee that I hated, so that I might understand the taste that the grown-ups favoured. Then, even if he weren't here any more, I wouldn't be sad, I told myself—I *wouldn't be sad.*

'Dao Nhue.'

Hai Saeng was nudging my arm with his toe as I was lying in peace. 'Where are you off to? Uncle's said it's time to eat.'

'It's evening already?'

'Uh-huh.' At that, he turned around and led the way. I came to notice while following behind him that Hai Saeng's pitch-black hair was long enough to graze the base of his neck in the absence of trips to the hairdresser. Loose strands of hair around his ears curved along his face, his shoulders were broad, his body skinny and tall, and every portion of his face was much more flawlessly in place than ever before. In that one short summer, Hai Saeng had grown up a little bit more.

**29**

The upperclassmen once said that time turns faster when you are a third-year in junior high. Rainstorms came and went, replaced by the first wave of cold wind. Mid-December, Hai Saeng and I applied for T school's entrance exam with his uncle offering to drive us there and back. Many teenagers my age came to apply for the exam in person; as for me, having only been half-heartedly studying, I only came to feel the pressure from that mass of people right on that day. All these people would be sitting in a giant convention hall only for a special few among them to be selected. I felt chills and glanced over with uncertainty at Hai Saeng—only to find that he was sitting still, unfazed.

Or to be precise, he didn't care about them at all.

'Aren't you afraid?' I whispered.

'Afraid of what? It's just an exam registration.'

'There's a lot of people—your science programme only accepts 700 students.'

Hai Saeng smiled. 'That can't be helped.'

The last week of December, we celebrated Christmas and New Year's Eve in one go on the last Friday of the year. Mom's cook-to-order restaurant was decorated with red and green garlands, and there was a fake, small Christmas tree with gold baubles and a small Santa Claus in the middle of the restaurant. I looked at the result of my decoration skill with pride. However, the old radio that Mom had in her restaurant was still playing Thai oldies as always. Hearing the lyrics that went, '*Birds are in love, in love with but sweet words, unlike humans with their vile, lying tongues,*' instead of 'Jingle Bells' had turned off many customers' mood for winter.

Normally, Hai Saeng and I didn't have any gift-exchanging custom; my small room was too suffocating to store any big articles, and whenever Hai Saeng wanted anything, he would buy it for himself with the money from his bank account that his parents took turns adding more to every month. However, with this being our last junior high year, Hai Saeng came up with the idea that we should get presents for each other as per the holiday custom.

'What would you like, then?' I asked.

'Guess.'

'Any rules?'

'There is.' Hai Saeng pressed his finger on his lips in a shushing gesture. 'You can't buy it with money.'

What a naughty rule, as expected of him. I knew right away what he wanted—no wonder we had always been on Santa Claus' naughty list and undeserving of presents. Still, could I ever go against his wishes?

I put on my hoodie and sauntered around the market, looking for any gift shops or stationery stores with a blind spot to sneak stuff into my pocket. Market communities within our province rarely had security cameras, and shopkeepers were usually some old grannies nodding off behind the counter; I only needed to choose something that he might like.

I looked at flowers and shook my head—Hai Saeng never cared for flowers unless he was picking them to throw them away in boredom—that choice was crossed out almost instantly. What else, plush toys? I imagined him using one as a target to throw knives at and felt pain in its stead. Notebook? Paper? Fountain pen?

Not bad. A nice, black fountain pen would suit him well. I thought back to when we rode my bicycle near that chess table and swiped the horse piece back with us. Hai Saeng was telling me in whispers what he wanted, to which I complied. We took what we wanted when the adults were turning the other way around, then ran away—*What an easy job*, I thought. My mind was set on a fountain pen case behind the glass showcase. I was about to snatch it, and that was when I saw the reflection of a fifteen-year-old boy in that showcase.

I was no longer eight years old.

Fear ran to my right hand, its touch freezing cold. My hand was bereft of power right at that instant. If I were to steal something as a rackety kid and was caught, I might be scolded—at worst, whipped, or the shop owner would have my parents pay in recompense. However, if it were a fifteen-year-old boy who had planned to shoplift with his full conscience, the shop owner might consider reporting to the police. At best, I would be fined; at worst, what would it be? Correctional institution? Juvenile detention centre? I was no longer eight years old. If I were to make mistakes now, no one would forgive me any more.

'*When childhood dies, its corpses are called adults*'—a British writer's words that Hai Saeng once quoted drifted into my mind. Fear spread through my whole body, its course pumped through my heart. I hesitated. I felt fear. It was not the fear of the results or punishments, but rather the fear of time that rushed past at an alarming speed.

I couldn't believe that youth was such a convenient thing. I couldn't believe that one day, we wouldn't be who we once were any more.

### 30

At night, once the time we agreed upon arrived, Hai Saeng and I met up at a swing set in the village's dumping ground.

'Merry Christmas, Dao Nhue,' Hai Saeng greeted me when he spotted me.

'Merry Christmas, Hai Saeng.'

'Is that your present? How big.'

'Actually,' I smiled awkwardly, feeling somewhat ashamed. 'I tried to shoplift a fountain pen, but, like, I didn't make it—I didn't have enough courage—so I brought you something from my home instead.'

'Ah.' Hai Saeng didn't mock my sudden cowardice. He craned his neck to look at what I had brought. 'What did you bring, then?'

I handed him the golf club that I had brought with me. It was big, unwieldy, and heavy with its metallic body. 'I snuck this out of my dad's storage room. He hasn't played golf in years because of bad knees.'

Hai Saeng raised his brow. 'What should I do with it, then, my dear Dao Nhue?'

'I thought you might want it.' I came up with the reason out of thin air at that moment, sweat trickling down my temple. 'A good-luck charm that fits your hands better than a small ashtray.'

What sorry reasoning. What did I say? 'Fits the hands better than an ashtray'—what's that? Hai Saeng was taken aback for a moment, then a corner of his lips curved into a smile. He took the golf club. 'Thank you,' he said as he reached into his pocket and placed something small into my hand.

'This one's yours.'

I held out my hand. On it, a small metal key, its shape unremarkable.

'What's this key for?' I asked.

'For the mailbox right in front of my house,' he answered. 'Don't open it until summer next year.'

'Huh, then this isn't a Christmas present?'

'The key's your Christmas present; the thing in that mailbox your summer present. I know you're good at waiting, so can you wait for two more months?'

'Wait. You brought this key from your house too. Didn't you make that rule to have us steal stuff?'

'When did I tell you to steal?' My face went red from having been fooled. Hai Saeng looked at my face and laughed. 'Hey, I'm glad you told me outright that you couldn't steal—not a problem at all, really. Are you ashamed of being a good person with a good conscience?'

'Don't pull my leg, Hai Saeng. I . . . I was really afraid.'

I didn't know why tears welled up in my eyes once I said this sentence. I looked the other way and hurriedly rubbed those hot droplets away with my wrist. 'It's embarrassing—really embarrassing. Don't look,' I mumbled in my throat. My tears wouldn't stop. I didn't understand what was happening—why was the fear that kept me from stealing today leaving such an impact on me? Hai Saeng observed me in silence and stillness, then stood up to embrace me. We went back to his house, walked past the piano in the main hall, and headed to his room on the second floor where we huddled beneath a blanket that embraced us like a riverside bird's nest. I continued to weep in Hai Saeng's arms, till the new year's fireworks lit the whole sky ablaze.

## 31

March, on the last day of our final exam, ninth graders were hugging each other, saying goodbyes as if they weren't going to see one another again, when in fact at least half of them would still be going to the same school; there was just a handful of those who made it through high school entrance exams for famous schools in Bangkok. Our provincial school wasn't known for outstanding education, with some students (me included) more interested in pursuing a vocational degree rather than the usual academic degree. I was eyeing the provincial vocational school, but I didn't tell Mom just yet—she really hoped that I would get into T high school.

As for me? I knew my fate right away when I first turned the page to the English exam.

There was this weird tradition that T high school's entrance exam result would be posted on a board next to the basketball court one night before the announcement, and the parents would sneak up to the board and look for the name of their children using flashlights. Nowadays, the result could be checked online using one's mobile phone, but Uncle H was among those who drove to the city just to see his nephew's exam result with his own eyes.

'Dao Nhue, you got 421st place,' Hai Saeng read his uncle's message out loud as we were sitting side-by-side on the piano stool.

'So, did I make it?'

'Your arts-maths programme seems to accept only 120 students. You're placed around the median of all examinees.'

I laughed, regretting the result and feeling relieved at the same time. The hellhole of English exercises was finally over and done with. Mom might be disappointed, but that couldn't be helped—the summer break that awaited us was much more exciting.

I continued to ask, 'What about you?'

'Second.'

'Second what?'

Hai Saeng raised his brow, his voice nonchalant. 'I got second place.'

'Whoa!' I stood right up. 'The second place! That's so cool!'

'You don't seem to believe it.'

'I knew that you would make it, but who would have thought that you'd be in the top three? Our school's going to put your face on a huge vinyl screen.' I was thrilled. Hai Saeng listened to me and yawned, then continued to play the piano again. He had been learning how to play 'Kiss the Rain' with its slow, sweet, and moving rhythm unlike any he had ever played before. I couldn't tell from Hai Saeng's indifferent face whether he was happy with the result or not. Of course, Hai Saeng poured all he had into studying and taking exams, but I had never once got any answers out of him about what he thought of the capital city. Which did he prefer? 'Of course,' he answered me thus long ago. Just 'of course' he would make it through the exam. But what was next?

Whatever, he would leave once summer ended anyway. I rested my head against his shoulder and prayed for a long summer that was packed full of stories.

## 32

Sunday, around four in the morning, I woke up feeling paralysed. Something heavy was sitting on top of my chest, making me unable to take a breath. I tried to open my eyes, then I saw a familiar silhouette staring back at me, glossy back hair covering the face, a pair of wide eyes, and a wide grin.

'Hai Saeng,' I whispered.

'It's a ghost, boo! Are you scared now?' He said in a raspy voice.

'You're heavy,' I said. Hai Saeng refused to get up. I moved for him to scoot away from my chest just so I could have an easier time breathing. Then I asked, 'How did you get inside my house?'

'Lock picking, of course.' Hai Saeng smiled. He was in his casual clothes with a long-sleeve shirt, a cap, and his same old rucksack. 'You have fifteen minutes to put away your stuff, Dao Nhue. Our summer has begun. Tell no one else. Go.'

'Wait, why does it have to be so early? Where are we going?' I rubbed my eyes drowsily.

Hai Saeng leaned closer in and whispered softly, 'The horizon.'

Then, I was wide awake. Just that one word alone was enough to have me abandon everything else and follow him.

We rode the motorbike to the terminal station for vans, asked a nearby grocery store to look after the motorbike for us, then took a van heading to Bangkok. I had never travelled in Bangkok public transport before, so Hai Saeng was the one who guided me on to buses and trains—what a busy and bustling city it was. Then we arrived at Hua Lamphong train station where you could buy a northbound ticket to Chiang Mai. After that, we had a meal in the station and ample time to waste away until 2.30 p.m. An announcement saying that trains from all platforms would be delayed had me furrow my brows.

'Is this kind of delay normal?' I asked when we were on our train at last. The train moved at a leisurely speed, bringing us further away from the grey metropolitan and closer to the rural area.

'Yeah,' Hai Saeng answered. 'How cool, right?'

'Really cool.'

'Have you ever travelled north?'

'Never.'

'Neither have I. I heard you only need to travel an hour by plane, but, if it's a train, you would have as many as twelve hours where you could do nothing but sit still.'

I laughed. 'What are we gonna do once we arrive?'

Hai Saeng rested his chin on his hand atop the table's surface. No answer was provided. We ate tuna sandwiches and drank orange juice that we bought from the station for a light meal, then we sat lounging around and nodding off time after time.

'Did you check the mailbox already?' Hai Saeng asked, swallowed by the sunset's orange shadow.

'Not yet. Is it urgent?'

'No.'

'What's in there?'

'I'm not telling you.' He smiled. 'Take a guess.'

## 33

I kept my phone turned off during the first day of our trip. We arrived at Chiang Mai train station near ten in the morning. 'Who said twelve hours again?' I grumbled. The Bangkok-Chiang Mai train took eighteen hours in total, and it had been held up in Lampang for very long.

'There's no need to hurry. We have a lot of time on our hands,' Hai Saeng answered, chuckling.

Then, we headed outside to catch a bus to Chiang Rai. 'It's much quieter and cheaper over there,' Hai Saeng suggested. I had no objection. We didn't have much to do last night apart from stargazing, and there weren't that many stars; there was too much light pollution from the cities. 'If we really want to stargaze, we have to climb up the mountain,' I said. Hai Saeng shrugged.

We hopped on to the bus bound for Chiang Rai as soon as the ticket office was open, then we rented a motorbike and checked the city out. Chiang Rai always had tourists during winter, while summer was somewhat quieter, which, fortunately, meant vacant guesthouses at cheaper price. We found a house along the Kok

River, located not too far from the city. It was made of pale-yellow wood and zinc plates and seemed to have served as a garage before. Inside were retro curtains that were once popular two decades ago, a fake Persian carpet hung on the wall alongside a framed poster of The Beatles, two small beds, and a ceiling fan. Hai Saeng headed inside to ask for the price. After a short talk with the owner, he concluded that it was 'not bad'. He handed the house owner his ID card—his legit card this time around—and thus it was concluded that we would stay there until we had the next plan.

However, neither of us liked to make plans. We spent our days sleeping, going to the market for some food, and going to bookstores. There was a day where we rode until we reached some corporate agricultural area, then we walked around and headed back, made love, slept, and woke up to make love once more. My body seemed to know in advance that we didn't have much of such time left, so it yearned without end for him—Hai Saeng, too. 'Dao Nhue,' he called my name as we lay atop each other in the stillness just beyond the curtains. 'Dao Nhue'—these words sounded beautiful and bursting with sparkles once uttered through his lips.

The mid-March sky was glaring in a way we hadn't seen in a while. From our bedroom window, I could see the riverbank, the river's gentle stream—its water level going down in summer—and dragonflies soaring up high. Hai Saeng was sleeping in the bed, his eyelashes resting still atop his cheeks, making him look like a small angel. *How could I live these past six summers without him?* I wondered to myself. Then, I realized that we hadn't contacted our families ever since we had left. My mom had long stopped complaining about how we often sneaked out for small outings and had already given up on my test result too. I reckoned that I should give her a call to let her know that we'll be staying here for a while to spare her needless worries. I turned on my phone and found a ton of missed calls, one of which was my mom's; as for the rest, they were Uncle H's.

Uncle H was losing his mind because of us again, it seemed. What a pitiful cousin he was. I had no plan to call him back, but while I was scrolling through the rest of those lengthy missed calls, Uncle H called me again. Caught by surprise, I accidentally answered the call. A long sigh was first to pierce through, followed by an earth-shattering yell.

'Where in Thailand are you two?!'

I rubbed my ear and lowered the volume, then tried my best to talk to him calmly. 'We are on a trip, like always. There's nothing to worry about, Uncle.'

'Like hell it is—did Saeng not tell you anything?!'

'Yes? Tell me what?'

'Arrrgh!' Uncle was going crazy for real. 'Nong Nhue, listen to me! Listen! Do you know what day it was when both of you disappeared?' he asked, and, without waiting for my answer, he continued right away. 'New student enrolment day, that's what it was! Thank God it could be filled online, so I did it for him already. But today, Nong Nhue, is T school's on-site enrolment day. Every new student must be there physically or their name is removed from the registry otherwise, and both of you decided to disappear. Where is Saeng? Are you guys in Bangkok? Well, let's meet up at the school right away!'

'About that, I don't think it's possible.'

'What do you mean?'

'So, we are . . .'

*Beep—*

The mobile phone was no longer in my hand. Hai Saeng took it away in one smooth swipe, hung up the call, and muttered, 'How noisy—I'm still sleepy here.'

I didn't quite know how to react to this.

'Hai Saeng, what did Uncle H mean by that?'

'Hmm?' he groaned.

'Is today the student enrolment day at your school?'

'Uh-huh.'

'And?'

'Don't fret over it, Dao Nhue.' Hai Saeng smiled, his eyes sparkling like a pond caught under sunlight. 'I promised to pass the exam, but I said nothing about actually going to that school, no?'


## 34

Revenge is a dish best served cold.

'I would like one large serving of this, please. What are you having, Dao Nhue?'

'Hmm . . . An affogato.'

'Ice cream with coffee poured on top? I didn't know you drank coffee.'

'I don't. I just want to try it.'

More than a year ago, before I had got into a fight with Uncle H and had run away to Bang Tabun together with Hai Saeng—no, it had actually been before that— ever since he had told me for the first time, just before the October semester break, that his mom wanted him to study at T school. Ever since back then, back when I could do nothing but get angry and feel suffocated in lieu of him, it was out of everyone's grasp, with that sarcastic tone in his reply completely looked over—'*Of course*'—that Hai Saeng's plan had long begun.

To place among the top ranks to get everyone elated, then snuff out their dreams entirely.

With a long-handled silver spoon, Hai Saeng enjoyed his eight scoops of lime sorbet from a large parfait bowl at a leisurely speed, one spoonful after another. I watched him eat, and what a nice scenery it was. We sat at a small coffee table in an all-homemade riverside ice cream parlour next to the Kok River. Trees on either side of the river were shedding their dry, yellow leaves amid scorching breezes. Golden shower trees bloomed in garish yellow, one of their tiny petals falling into my affogato cup, which I picked out without nary a complaint.

'How's your coffee?' Hai Saeng asked.

'Not bad if you have it with ice cream, but I still wouldn't have it by itself—I don't really understand all this bitterness.'

'Oh dear, you're still a baby after all.'

'We are the same age.' I smiled.

It had been three days ever since the day Hai Saeng had hung up on Uncle H. We were still spending our time leisurely in Chiang Rai as if nothing had happened. I asked Hai Saeng what he would do next with his high school path, would he stay at the same school, and would his parents allow him to. Hai Saeng always brushed it off in mild annoyance, saying, 'I'll think about that later,' or, 'We're on a trip, why talk about serious stuff?' I admired Hai Saeng's coolness. Someone as equipped with skills and wealth as him seemed to have his future secured. Taking a year off from school wouldn't trouble him—he didn't care about what others said anyway.

What I wondered about was such a minuscule matter it was nearing trivial: I wanted to know what Hai Saeng felt towards those around him—towards Uncle H who earnestly loved and cared about him, at least. Hai Saeng wanted to get back at his dad and mom, but what about his uncle? He got to enjoy a mountain of ice cream like he had wanted, but did he have no mind to explain to other concerned parties what he did all this for? This question sounded extremely contradictory coming from me, someone who wanted Hai Saeng to stay in our tiny town for as long as possible. It seemed I was more sympathetic towards Uncle H than I had originally thought I was.

I asked that question, and Hai Saeng answered thus:

'Why should I explain it?'

'Because Uncle loves you. He wants to understand you.'

'I didn't do it out of love.' He rested his chin on his elbow. 'I didn't ask Uncle to love me; I want everyone to get the heck away.'

I was taken aback by his words. I continued to ask, strenuously, 'Does that include me?'

'You what?'

'Are you happy that I love you? Do you want to be with me? Do my feelings for you make you feel burdensome?'

Hai Saeng furrowed his brows. Once he understood the questions that pointed towards a slighted heart, he sighed weakly. 'I'm sorry. Don't ask me—I don't know what to do.'

'Hai Saeng.'

'I have only ever known anger and fear.' Hai Saeng looked upward at a golden shower tree as its branches yielded to the hot breeze, his eyes reflecting nothing—void and still. 'Even now, all the anger that has been buried ever since I was a mere child never faded away. As days pass by, it only turns into a time bomb. I've exacted it—if you're putting it that way—I've exacted my revenge, but I'm not satisfied, nor do I know how to achieve that. It won't ever end, Dao Nhue. This is all your fault.'

'My fault?'

'That night.' He smiled a gentle smile, his hand stroking my knuckles tenderly. 'If only you had killed me that night.'

## 35

After a week or so had passed since we left for our run-away trip, we headed back home. It was not because we ran out of money, felt insecure, or missed our usual beddings this time around, but it was due to Uncle's H unceasing calls that I couldn't stand it any more. My gut was telling me that we might have overstepped the boundaries. 'Uncle H is probably so anxious his whole head's turned grey now,' I told Hai Saeng. He shrugged.

'You can call him back,' he permitted me nonchalantly.

My gut was right. We made Uncle H cry.

'I was worried about you two!' He started off with that right away. 'You guys are unbelievable, doing things as if there are just the two of you in this whole world—do you never care about how others might feel? Why do you have to resort to running away? I didn't even know that Saeng didn't want to go to school in Bangkok—why wouldn't you tell me anything?'

Uncle H talked in a such a rapid flood that it was hard to make sense of what he said.

'I already told you,' I whispered.

'You never did! You told me that I should allow that kid to make his own choices, and how was I supposed to know what Saeng wanted—he never agreed to or denied anything at all—ARGH! That doesn't matter any more, the enrolment date has already passed. Hey, you guys don't have to go in hiding any more. I beg you, please come back,' Uncle said while sobbing. I imagined that he must be blowing his nose at the same time too. A sniffing noise was caught by the microphone. 'Saeng, Nong Nhue, can't we start anew? I won't scold you at all, and we won't talk about this again, but can you two open up to me, just the tiniest bit, from now on?'

The guilt crashed upon me like a tsunami. I felt my eyes brimming with tears.

I looked at Hai Saeng. 'Your uncle really loves you, you know.'

He looked the other way, trying his darndest to seem as nonchalant as before, but I could see that he was swayed as well. He said, 'It's up to you.'

I looked back at the phone and stroked it gently, wishing that the warmth from my hand could travel all the way to pat Uncle H on his back too, just in case it might help him to stop crying. 'Uncle,' I said softly, 'I'm sorry for worrying you. We'll be coming back home now.'

We travelled from Chiang Rai to Bangkok with a low-cost airline. Uncle H came to pick us up at Don Muang airport in a quite sorry state. His neatly combed hair seemed to have some stray grey strands, and his eyes were sunken like someone who hadn't slept. Uncle H must have cried before he came here, but he didn't complain. I had prepared myself mentally to be scolded for a bit, but he said nothing when he saw us; he simply helped us put the baggage in the car and drove home in silence. Uncle H dropped me off at my home before heading back to his.

'I'm really sorry, Uncle,' I repeated just before I got out of the car.

'I know.' Uncle H smiled. 'You're a lot like me when I was young, Nong Nhue. Sometimes I feel as if I'm seeing myself—stubborn, with no ill will.'

Uncle's voice made me want to cry again. 'I think that Hai Saeng also has lots of things he wants to talk to you about.' I looked at the backseat. Hai Saeng was pretending to be asleep, likely annoyed that his name was mentioned.

'That kid never told me anything, be it his happiness, sadness, or anger pent up inside,' Uncle H replied. 'I know that he's always angry, but I don't know its cause—

never. I tried making our house nice to live in, livening up the mood just in case he would be happy, preparing good food for him at home, but Saeng only wanted to run away with you.'

'That's not your fault, Uncle.'

'I do wish I were younger, then maybe he would tell me, too, what he was actually running away from.'

Uncle H smiled weakly. I, on the other hand, couldn't bring myself to smile, thinking that it would be best for him if he remained ignorant over certain matters. Being an overthinker in a family ridden with the past, he might never see them in the same light ever again.

I looked at Hai Saeng, still pretending to be asleep with his eyes closed, and whispered quietly next to his ear, 'See you tomorrow.' Hai Saeng nodded. I looked on as their car headed into a deep alley, going back to the haunted house at the foot of the hills.

The day might come—the day where Hai Saeng opens his heart to others—this, I hope with all my heart. Summer at the fork of our lives glimmered beautifully. This exact point in life is where children our age ought to have a heart filled with hope.

I must have forgotten that we couldn't possibly wish for the summer sky to remain ever sunny; as when the weather has remained sunny for so long that the land is arid, what would hit our small town next is a storm.

## 36

Before a storm, there is a sign known as 'the calm'—the calm before the storm. Everything was going well without me ever noticing that it might be our last moment. Uncle H brought Hai Saeng and I to the sea, waterfall, and national park for its natural trails. He stopped lecturing us to stay at home prim-and-properly, stopped badgering us to partake in *normal activities of normal teenagers*. From that day onward, whenever he noticed that we were preparing to head out on a trip, he would offer to bring us to places himself. At first, Hai Saeng was annoyed by this, but that was only until the day he saw Uncle H sneaking a cigarette between his lips as he sat in his car alone, the two of us stargazing on a reed mat outside.

'Do you smoke too?' he said. Uncle H jumped like a rabbit smacked with a morning glory stalk on its bum.

'Yikes, Saeng! Don't tell your mom!'

Hearing that, Hai Saeng grinned and held out his hand. 'Give me one to keep my mouth shut.'

Then they stood leaning against the car's hood, blowing wisps of white smoke everywhere. Uncle H held the cigarette smoke within his mouth, then blew it out in round doughnuts and ended up coughing non-stop, his hands clutching his stomach. Hai Saeng said to him, 'And you were acting all cool.' I laughed as I lay there looking at them. I had never seen Hai Saeng opening up to Uncle H to that extent before. The sky was clear that night, sprinkled with stars. The three of us lay on the ground and talked to each other with Uncle H doing the most talking. He told us stories from when he was young.

'I used to ride a big bike going from north to south with my friends. We had to stay away from the police's exhaust smoke checkpoints along the way. Things weren't as easy as it is today, but it was much more serene. We could even ask folks along the way to stay overnight at their place, but my friend was snoring so loud that we got kicked out in the middle of the night. Man . . . back then, I didn't get to wash my hair for two weeks or so, and my hair got so oily. My skin was also burnt shades darker because I wore this sun-absorbing leather jacket. When I got home, my sister almost didn't let me inside—she couldn't remember her little brother.'

'If you were so unruly before, how come you turned into such a worrywart?' I asked.

'Because I believed back then that the world was ours, when in fact it isn't.' Uncle H seemed saddened when he had to answer thus. 'From my perspective when I was young, I only wanted to have fun. But when I look back now that I'm grown up, well, what did I do? How darn dangerous, poor parents—once you realize that, you wouldn't want your own nieces and nephews to risk their lives the same way that you did. But it's useless trying to forbid them, right, Saeng? I have to let you grow.'

'Yes,' Hai Saeng answered. 'You have to let us die.'

'Ugh, you're unbelievable.'

We laughed.

Uncle H told us that you would see the sky if you were to look up when you were young, but adults would see a ceiling. 'The grown-ups' world isn't in the least bit gentle. I get to run my own bar, and I'm among the fortunate ones who get to pursue their dreams, but I always suffer from these pains without cause. My head's filled with thoughts of loss and revenue, relationships, having to please others, and I couldn't stop thinking about all this even if I tried. Childhood friends that were once cool in my eyes all turned into the same kind of adults—bored and withered in the city where we had to scrounge happiness from good food and films just to sleep another night.'

'Then, when you said that the bar's temporarily closed . . .'

'Uh-huh. With this state of mind, I couldn't continue to keep it open, so I closed up the place. Actually, I was the one who offered to stay with you in this town. It was I who begged your mom, but I wouldn't be so believable if I said so from the start, no? How could I, who couldn't even take care of himself, take care of others? You two are way more precocious compared to children your age, especially Nong Nhue, always going wherever your friend asks. And Saeng's even picked up smoking, still . . .' Uncle H smiled. 'I'm very happy.'

I was happy too. I looked at Hai Saeng. He was pretending to be asleep. Hai Saeng always did that when he didn't want to reveal his true feelings—he was just like that. I reached out to hold his hand. We lit a mosquito-repelling incense and placed it near our feet, then lay there underneath a blanket of moonlight and a mosquito mesh woven from silver stars. The three of us were very happy back then.

## 37

I should have known, like all those rural villagers who had this shared clairvoyance whenever something strange slipped into the village. I should have known when I first saw that gorgeous white Mercedes. It was in no way blending in with houses from the housing estate where people around here lived in, all in the same shape, varied in colours, and modestly decorated. There were only a few of those in our alley who owned a car, and such a luxurious car with a wide square-shaped front only looked like a foreign being that sucked all our air into its lungs. I should have stopped it before the car's owner could park it in front of the haunted house at the end of the alley. I should have stopped it with whatever someone insignificant like me was capable of. Before I came to realize that this would be the last scene in our story, all starring characters were already placed in front of the camera.

Two in the afternoon, when the temperature reached its peak, I stood in front of Hai Saeng's house, then squeezed myself in to unlock the rusty front gate, sandwiched between the gate and a huge car that was parked, blocking it. At first, I thought that Uncle H had a guest from Bangkok visiting him, then I realized just a few minutes later that it wasn't the case. The house's cheerful air turned unusually sombre on that day. It was 35 degrees Celsius without a single cloud in the sky, and I hoped that it would rain just in case that might help with the heat. I walked past the front where I spotted one extra pair of shoes, and reached the back door that I always entered and left the house through—Uncle H always left this door open to allow breezes of air to pass through the house during the day. Once I reached the kitchen inside the house, I heard people talking from within the dining room.

One of the voices belonged to Uncle H, seemingly agitated: 'Calm down, let's talk through this calmly, please, you two?'

The second one was Hai Saeng's, nonchalant, apathetic: 'But I have nothing to talk about.'

The third voice was one I had never heard before, but I knew that I detested this condescending tone of voice: 'It was thoughtless of me to have allowed you to stay with my son, Hirun. You should have disciplined him, but this—you doted on him so much the kid's turned into a spoiled brat. I'm not going to let this matter pass.'

Well, now we know Uncle H's real name, but I reckon it wouldn't be of much use now. Let's just imagine that Uncle Hirun, Hai Saeng, and Hai Saeng's dad were all sitting at the same table at that moment. My guess is that Hai Saeng must be sitting with his feet on the table, or perhaps chewing a piece of gum with this most annoying air to him, hence the reason his dad was so mad. As for me, I still couldn't muster enough courage to move from where I was standing—to step forward or to retreat were two equally suffocating choices.

'I'll say this again,' Hai Saeng's dad said. 'Saeng, you'll attend T school whether you like it or not.'

'The enrolment date has long passed,' Hai Saeng replied. I didn't see his expression, but I imagined it was as void of emotion as ever.

'I'll talk to someone on the inside. Your mother knows a lot of alumni, and with your ranking score, the school board will certainly listen.'

'Through bribing? Wow.'

'Don't you act all high and mighty. Who is it that forced us to do this?' Hai Saeng's dad said through gritted teeth, his shame tangible. 'You passed the entrance exam of a nice school in Bangkok in seventh grade, but you wanted to study in other provinces no matter what anyone else said. I paid all that I could for you, because your mother blamed it on me. You must be making delinquent friends again, aren't you? You let them fill your head with unruly ideas—that must be it—someone like you couldn't come up with all this stuff on your own, I didn't teach you to become like this.'

Hai Saeng's dad began blaming it on others. It was like they said: parents want their children to obey them at all times, otherwise they'll feel as if they're losing control over them. This adult's tone of voice, too, was shaking from anger. A *guilty conscience needs no accuser*, I thought. He could only bring this and that up to bury away his own wrongdoings in the past.

'I thought you and Mother wanted me to stay away, out of your sight. Why play the role of the best parent ever now, worrying so much about my future?'

'What are you talking about? You mother and I only want our family to be as good as it was again. You never see others' efforts, do you? You're the one who pushes others away—never happy with anything we gave you. What's the problem with you, really?'

Hai Saeng replied, 'The problem is, I detest you and Mother.'

That made Uncle Hirun take a sharp breath so audibly, it reached my ears. He didn't know the cause of all this yet, but he was about to. Everything would change if he did, which was the truth Hai Saeng's dad knew full well. That man hated having his crimes revealed above all else. When Hai Saeng was young, he didn't tell anyone about what he fell victim to apart from his mom, who told him to keep quiet and never tell anyone. She was no less afraid of having her family's name tarnished. Both of them hid their loathsome pasts at the bottom of a deep pond, a black pond in a boy's shape. And now, the voice of a grown-up boy was shaking them so hard they couldn't remain seated.

I sensed that Hai Saeng must be smiling at that moment. This was the moment he had long awaited his whole life.

'I detest you and Mother, is that clear?' Hai Saeng said cooly. 'I don't want to see the both of you ever again. Just imagining that I have to sit all smiley at a dining table with you makes me want to throw up right away.'

'Hai Saeng!' Uncle Hirun chided him.

'You shut your mouth, Saeng.'

'I can, if you would grace me with an answer: You keep going on about mending our family and all that, but pray tell me how our family fell apart?'

'Because of you,' Hai Saeng's dad said through gritted teeth. 'If not for you, everything would have remained the same.'

'Because of me?' Hai Saeng's voice perked up as if he had just heard an interesting conspiracy theory. He clapped his hands before continuing, 'Do you remember this, Father?' He then placed something on to the table, two hard surfaces making a soft thudding sound. Unable to contain my curiosity any longer, I peeked out. It was his good-luck charm—the ashtray made of crystal glass. Uncle Hirun furrowed his brows, unable to make sense of what he saw, while the expression Hai Saeng's dad had on his face distorted noticeably.

He said with a shaking voice, unable to contain his emotions, 'What the hell are you doing?'

'Do you remember what happened? If you don't, let me renew your memory.'

'That was so many years ago. I have been taking good care of you since then.'

'How self-assured.'

'At least you never go hungry. There are so many kids on the streets that don't have the same opportunity you do, but you threw it all away as if all the good things we gave you are worth nothing.'

'Did those kids on the streets . . .' Hai Saeng placed his hand atop the other on the table's surface, ' . . . face the same thing you did to me?'

'Wait a minute, please, what is this all about?' Uncle Hirun spoke up.

'You stay out of this, Hirun!'

'Oh, Father dear, why do you talk to Uncle like that? He has all the rights to know. You want to know, right, Uncle? So, back then, Father loved me so much, maybe too much.'

'Shut up!'

'I was only a few years old.'

'Hai Saeng.' His dad glared at him, his hands clenched on the table, defeated. 'What do you want?'

Hai Saeng's pair of eyes that were as black as a deep pond narrowed.

He had been waiting for this question.

'Well, I have been asking myself all this time, too, about what I really want. Now that you asked me, I finally know the answer.' Silence enveloped the whole house. Hai Saeng stared into his dad's eyes. 'That after all this time, I have never heard an apology from you even once.'

## 38

A suffocating atmosphere held the dining room in its tight grip. Uncle Hirun seemed to finally understand the big picture of all this. Hai Saeng sat still with one hand on top of the other, calmly waiting. As for his dad, a rush of different emotions travelled through the veins on his face, angry one minute, afraid the other. This man had played all his cards, but his son remained undisturbed.

After a long moment of staring each other, the father said wearily, 'Saeng, has it never occurred to you that I might be suffering too?' He clenched his hands, his nails digging into the palms of his hands. Uncle Hirun stood up from his chair and patted his back, trying to help him deliver his words calmly. The man didn't deny the goodwill this time around. 'Ever since that incident, everything changed. Your mother avoids me and blames every small thing on me. Do you think that I chose for things to turn out like this? Do you think that I'm happy? I think every day that I want to turn back time to fix things, but that's impossible. The mistake from that day been haunting me year after year too. That's why I try to give you nice things.'

Hai Saeng looked at his dad's face, the look in his eyes not in the least bit softer. His dad was asking for mercy that he didn't deserve, and Hai Saeng was absolutely never going to grant him that mercy. 'I'll say this again, that after all this time, I have never once heard an apology from you.'

The father gritted his teeth this time around. 'So, you're going to do it like this? I'm your father, you know.'

'And?'

'Hirun, you haven't taught my son to respect his elders at all. No wonder he grew up to be so cocky,' Hai Saeng's dad started shifting the blame.

Uncle Hirun bowed his back down and tried to convince him otherwise, 'Please, my brother-in-law, I think that saying sorry to a child when we really wronged them isn't such a bad thing. You came all this way to reconcile with Saeng, didn't you? Saeng is actually a good kid and not that stubborn at all. If you ever made him so sad that it's ingrained in his head, just a sorry wouldn't be too much, would it?'

Hai Saeng remained still, making no remarks. I saw that calm dark water in his eyes—he was gauging the situation. What Hai Saeng's dad had done wasn't something that could be so easily forgiven with just an apology, of course. It was a crisis of faith that happened to one small kid and affected Hai Saeng's personality as he grew up, and in the long run turned that boy into a misfit, made him lack trust in others, and push everyone's goodwill away. Thus, what he asked from his dad wouldn't lead to forgiveness. He was only proving to Uncle Hirun and himself that even a well-deserved apology was too much to ask from his own father who was more willing to empty his wallet than hurt his pride—and Hai Saeng succeeded.

'All right,' Hai Saeng's dad said. 'I won't mess with your life again, is that what you want?'

Uncle Hirun stood stunned—this man wouldn't say sorry at all?

'Wait, brother-in-law, it's just . . .'

'You stand up so much for him, so take him as your own if you want, Hirun. Remember, I'll have nothing to do with him from this day onward.'

That sentence made Hai Saeng burst out laughing. I could no longer guess at this point which emotion was in control of Hai Saeng's heart—was he glad or angered, saddened or did he really find it humorous? This reaction from him, however, made his dad seethe in fury until his whole body was shaking. The man whipped around, adjusted his clothes, and was ready to leave this house.

Then I saw Hai Saeng, who was driven with no emotions whatsoever, who had already considered all angles and possibilities before carrying out the act. I thought back to the question he had asked me during our first night together, '*Dao Nhue, do you see me capable of murder?*'

Hai Saeng flicked his wrist once, then his favourite ashtray flew, aiming for the area just behind his dad's temple.

*Bullseye!*

### 39

*Do you see me capable of murder?*
*Do you think we could hide a body in our hideout?*
*I want Uncle to die, Mother, too. All of them should die. As for Father, I must be the one to kill him.*

*Will I be all right with killing him alone? I don't think so.*
*Too bad, but that'll have to be the next time.*

Whenever Hai Saeng said 'Killing Father', he never once joked.

The ashtray made from crystal glass landed at the perfect spot on his head. His dad's face turned to the side from the impact, then his body fell to the ground. He did not yell—it seemed to be so painful he was stunned. The one who cried at the top of his lungs, however, was Uncle Hirun. What happened in front of him was such a gruesome sight—one he never thought to see in this lifetime.

Hai Saeng watched as his good-luck charm fell to the ground and rolled away. He picked it up—the ashtray he threw around in the air to kill time, one that fit in his hand more perfectly than any other weapon. He approached his dad, raised it above his head, aiming at the same place, the final nail into the coffin. He would correct that mistake he once made when he was seven years old.

'Stop!'

Uncle Hirun interjected, trying his best to snatch that ashtray from his nephew's hand. With his adrenaline rush, Uncle was imbued with unusual strength. Hai Saeng didn't show much surprise on his face. Once he knew he wasn't capable of resisting that strength, he let go, and Uncle Hirun hurriedly threw the object the other way. He normally had this eye-rolling expression on, tired with his nephew's shenanigans, but it was today that I got to see fear on Uncle's face for the first time.

'Get a hold of yourself, Saeng. That's your dad—what were you going to do?' Uncle said, his voice pitchy; his body, trembling.

Hai Saeng narrowed his eyes, having no mind to argue with his uncle. Once disarmed, he turned around and headed for the under-stairs storage, ignoring a question unworthy of his answer. Hai Saeng's dad, clutching the area around his ear, stood up and said, 'You ungrateful brat, I dare you do that again.'

Uncle Hirun wanted to drop dead right there—why were the members of this family so eager to make matters worse, he must be thinking that. Uncle didn't know why Hai Saeng was heading for that storage and could only help the wounded up on his feet.

'Brother-in-law, Saeng is angry at the moment. I think you should flee now!'

'No. I'm gonna fucking teach him a lesson,' Hai Saeng's dad said even while limping. He walked fearlessly towards the storage. 'So full of yourself aren't you, you little fucker! Try that again, I dare you.'

That wasn't a smart idea—I should have warned him. I heard the doorknob to the storage turning, followed by a loud *thud*, one much louder than that of the ashtray just now. I heard Hai Saeng's dad howling in pain this time around. He took a step back, clutching one of his arms that was struck with full force by a boy with a weapon in hand. Hai Saeng's dad decided to not fight back any more. The middle-aged man grumbled and cursed his son while inching away with Hai Saeng slowly following after him, the golf club that I gave him as a Christmas present in his hands. He raised it all the way up with the gesture of a golfer preparing for a backswing, his eyes vacant. Uncle Hirun tried to stop him, but he couldn't reach them in time. Hai Saeng struck hard at the side of his dad's neck. Without allowing the middle-aged man any time to choke on his saliva, that pair of arms were rising up in the air again. He was aiming for the head this time.

'. . .!'

The golf club was stopped mid-air, held back by someone's hands. They weren't Uncle Hirun's.

They were mine.

I caught Hai Saeng in time, holding his arms back, preventing him from cutting the man's thread of life with his swing. Every pair of eyes was on me, wondering how long I had been taking part in the scene. I felt out of place, especially when I took Hai Saeng's expression into account— he seemed surprised and disappointed at the same time.

'Why are you stopping me? You of all people?' he mumbled in his throat, his voice low.

'I don't know. My hands moved on their own,' I replied, equally shocked.

'Let go.'

I was usually a tamed dog who always heeded to its master's order, but in that life-and-death moment, I yelled, 'Uncle! Hurry and take Hai Saeng's dad away!'

Uncle Hirun was still shocked. 'Nong Nhue, but . . .'

'Go!' I shouted, still trying my best to hold Hai Saeng's arms back. Uncle Hirun nodded and hurriedly carried the unconscious father by his arm and put him in Uncle's own car. I heard the car's engine going further away in the distance. Once they were out of Hai Saeng's pursuing distance, I finally let go of his arms.

I thought that Hai Saeng would charge forward and carry out what he began, but what I saw once I let go was him standing still, holding the golf club loosely in his hands, quiet.

He turned to look into my eyes. That pair of eyes was as sorrowful as that of a seven-year-old child who had lost his way.


## 40

'I have long been waiting for the day I get to kill Father. You know that don't you?'

Hai Saeng said as quietly as a whisper. I nodded, unable to meet his eyes.

'I know.'

'If you do, then why did you . . .'

'Killing him wouldn't make you feel any better.'

Hai Saeng turned to look at me, the bottom of his eyes quivering. 'I thought that you were the only one who understood me,' he said, putting on a fake smile, the kind that made me want to cry. 'Is it not, Dao Nhue? You were here, heard everything that man said to me, and you didn't understand? Or are you not on my side?'

'I didn't do it for your dad!' I grabbed his shoulders tightly. 'I'm on your side. I never once cared about which hole your dad would rot in. I hate him. Someone who hurt you—I'll never be on his side.'

'But you stopped me.'

'Hai Saeng, if you kill someone, we won't get to be together ever again,' I said, trying my darndest to keep my voice normal. It was, however, of no use—I was crying already. My throat was bitter with the lump of sadness stuck in it. Hai Saeng looked at me who was sobbing uncontrollably, then I saw him shedding a drop of tear. It was such a strange sight. Hai Saeng, in my eyes, was so strong I thought he didn't know how to cry. I hugged him. He sobbed, letting go of the weapon. We both wept and mourned for our childhood, one shattered by the hands of another.

'Hey, you. You never planned to help me hide the body from the beginning, did you?'

'I only went with the flow when you talked about this stuff, I never wanted to actually do it.'

Hai Saeng let out a soft sigh. 'Killing someone, that's all, right? The only thing you don't want me to do?'

I nodded. 'Just kill no one.'

'Then, what should I do? How can I quell this anger pent up inside without killing Father?'

'How do you usually deal with your anger?'

'I'm always angry. I do nothing. I just . . . watch.'

'Have you ever broken stuff?'

'I haven't.'

'Then…' After crying for a long while, we found ourselves in front of that most gorgeous Mercedes belonging to Hai Saeng's dad. Its owner had fled in Uncle Hirun's car and was most likely going to keep away from this place for a long time. Hai Saeng looked at the luxurious shape, which was worth some millions of baht, nonchalantly. I handed him the golf club and said, 'Go ahead.'

'Are you sure?'

'Of course.' I smiled; Hai Saeng, too. He raised the club above his head, and swung it down at the windshield, followed by the car's hood, tail lights, doors, then each and every window. He handed me the golf club. 'Become my accomplice now.' I took the club and swung it at the car's side-view mirror so hard it came off. Hai Saeng laughed softly. I looked at him. Tears didn't suit him. His smiling face was so gorgeous I wanted to cherish it.

'Do you feel better?' I asked.

'I never thought.' Hai Saeng stretched. 'I never thought it would feel this good.'

'Should have done it long ago, right?'

We headed to the second floor and dug through stuff Hai Saeng's parents didn't bring along and piled them up downstairs. I threw his mom's favourite pink glaze porcelain vase over to Hai Saeng, which he hit mid-air, shattering it into pieces. I looked for the next one. 'Which one do you want, your dad's necktie or his leather shoes?' Hai Saeng replied, 'Both.' He lit them up in fire right on the house floor, and we stomped on them before the fire would catch on other things. We took apart porcelain dolls, pushed chairs over, emptied silverware on to the floor and stomped on them, pulled at curtains until they fell off their rods. Our surroundings were turned into complete mayhem, nonetheless, we didn't touch a single thing that belonged to Uncle Hirun.

I thought back to what Mom said long ago.

*Buddha said that we should forgive our enemies—our anger will only eat away at us.*

*Those who did us wrong would have already forgotten about what they did, so why should we hold on to the grudge, dear?*

*When you grow up, you'll understand what I said, Nhue.*

Mom, if growing up means you'll lack empathy and see others' misfortunes as trivial matters that just happen to occur in your long life and blame it on the victims for how they can't forgive and forget, then I don't want to grow up at all. I want to take in his anger, all his sadness, and join him in this anger until he's ready to overcome his wounds of his own free will.

Forcing someone to forget or to forgive is really cruel, is it not?

Hai Saeng and I laid ourselves down among the broken remnants surrounding the upright piano. We didn't smash that piano, even though it belonged to Hai Saeng's mom.

'Uncle even went and restrung it—he would be sad if it's broken.'

Hai Saeng said so. I heard a crowd gathering in front of the house—perhaps nosy folks living in the area, that fortune-teller auntie and the chess uncle certainly among them. They would soon pour inside, unable to contain their curiosity and start shouting, 'Is anyone home? We heard a loud crash—is anyone injured?' Of course, they wouldn't really care about who was injured and whatnot— they only hungered for gossip, just like how they devoured their nightly soap operas. There, they began talking about the smashed-up car in front of the house.

Hai Saeng and I would be separated after this, of that I was certain. It was our fate.

But that's all right. We'll be all right. We'll find each other again. We'll always find each other again.

'It's just like back then,' Hai Saeng said with his eyes closed.

'Back then?'

'Our nest. Our secret hideout.'

'This one is too big to be a nest.'

'But it's messy enough, no?' He smiled. 'Filled with stuff, that is. Say, Dao Nhue, when all of this is over, let's think of which colour to paint the house with. I'm tired of Mother's wallpapers.'

'Uh-huh. I want a lime yellow kitchen.'

'Do you even know how to cook?'

'Is that important?'

'No.' Hai Saeng laughed. 'Pink house, green window frames, and black roof.'

'Is that Monet's house?'

'What does Monet's house look like?'

'Don't worry about it.'

'Yes, don't. I'm sleepy.'

'Let's take a nap together.'

'Uh-huh.'

*We'll be all right, Hai Saeng.* I held his hand under the dim sunlight, and we plunged down into a sweet slumber, the kind that we hadn't had for years.

**41**

Did you check the mailbox in front of my house?

I did.

Did you like the present?

'Nhue.' It was the voice of a female classmate sitting right next to me. She seemed to be annoyed even before the sun began to make its downward descent. 'Focus, don't use your phone—the exam's next week.'

'Of course, Mommy Joy,' I said cheekily.

'Who's your mom?' Joy kicked me in the leg. 'Your sweetheart decided to text you back now?'

'Yeah.'

'After how many days?'

'A week.'

'Wow. And you endure it? I'm this close to giving mine a break-up call when I'm left hanging even a single day.'

I laughed. 'It's normal, really, he just doesn't like texting.'

I went to the provincial vocational school instead of pursuing a normal high school degree. My mom didn't object when I chose to study in the culinary programme, only mumbling, sighing about how come I, someone who never stayed home for long, nor enjoyed talking to customers, would want to study culinary science just to help out at her restaurant in a rural, small village. Mom wanted me to go to Bangkok, telling me that a brighter future awaited me there. I, however, had never been known for my ambition.

I continued to live in that shabby room on the second floor of the local bistro, located at an alley near the foot of the hills where things remained forever unchanging. The world kept spinning, leaving this place behind. Its residents grew up. The younger ones left only to return once their hair turned grey. I looked on as the newer generation of primary school-goers rode their bicycles out in search of new adventures and built their own hideouts.

I had my own hideout too. It was left abandoned at the end of the alley, collecting dust with nary a soul wandering near.

On nights where I missed Hai Saeng (which I always did, it's just when my yearning for him was too great to bear in this case), I would leave with my old, trusty bicycle, then cut through the garbage dump and a gang of stray dogs on foot until I reached the house rumoured to be haunted. I would insert a key into the rusty padlock, and, behind that wooden door, there stretched our small world; therein lay a bowerbird's nest, filled with broken treasures that Hai Saeng and I had shattered with our own hands. Flowers once garnishing the vases were dried and withered, turning into dust. I could still vividly remember the day when the villagers stormed into this house. They were making all kinds of surprised noises and tried to shake us awake from our sweet summer dream, screaming, 'Nong Nhue, Saeng dear, what's happened here?!'—they had followed behind my mom, the world's second-most worried individual, with the world's most worried individual close behind: Uncle Hirun, who had just returned from bringing Hai Saeng's dad to the hospital. It was such a ruckus that Hai Saeng and I woke up to look at each other, then went back to sleep. Our two guardians shooed away those villagers afterwards.

We had to go our separate ways after that. Hai Saeng's house was left abandoned, while Uncle Hirun took Hai Saeng to stay with him in Bangkok. Hai Saeng got into an all-boys private high school as a special case (which was, as I heard, the result of a six-digit donation from Hai Saeng's mom). There was nothing to fret about when it came to his studies, but how he acted after that event. Uncle Hirun called to consult with me about that, bemoaning the circumstances, the sadness in his voice apparent.

'I don't know what I did wrong. That kid doesn't talk much, and he only spends his time all by himself in his room in the evening. Has he been calling you at all?'

'He hasn't,' I told him the truth. 'Please give him some time, Uncle, try not to rush him.'

'Does Saeng hate me, Nong Nhue? No one ever deigned to tell me what happened between that father and son. I only succeeded in nagging the answer out of my sister just now, so I understand at last what he has been angry about all along. It's terrible, really. I feel terrible for urging them to reconcile, knowing nothing whatsoever. If I were Saeng, I wouldn't know what to do.'

'Hai Saeng can't possibly hate you.' I laughed softly, thinking back to when we used the golf club to smash all his parents' belongings, but spared Uncle Hirun's piano. 'Hai Saeng's glad that you are around, he just won't accept his feelings just yet.'

I loved to sneak inside Hai Saeng's house and lay down on the floor, breathing in dust and smoke from bygone days, listening to the pitter-patter of rain just outside the window, imagining that it was the piano rendition of 'Kiss the Rain' that he liked to play, then cried from the pain of missing him. The house he used to live in, the bedroom once filled with his scent, the dreamy times when I could only steal a glance at him above an exercise book, and those sweet days when we never let time pass by without kissing and embracing one another.

Hai Saeng had never returned here ever since that incident. His dad sent someone to pick up the car, and never once asked about the son that tried to kill him ever again. His mom was furious when she found out about the mess that might affect her social standing. I had been sending him texts from time to time, checking in on him. Hai Saeng replied as curtly as always. He didn't like talking through text—they couldn't convey as much emotion compared to a face-to-face conversation, that much I knew.

Half a semester came and went; Uncle Hirun told me that Hai Saeng began opening up to him slowly.

'That boy's back to being disobedient again! When I told him that he doesn't have to meet his parents again, Saeng asked me, "*Can I go work at your bar at night from now on, then?*"—I reckoned having my nephew close to me would be better than having him roam the streets outside, so I said yes. Oh, Lord. He played pool against my customers and got thousands in tips!'

'Uncle, your workplace is a bar, and Hai Saeng's only in tenth grade. Wouldn't the police get him?'

Uncle Hirun replied in a sheepish voice. 'I'm afraid of that too. But it's Saeng we're talking about, you know.'

Of course, Hai Saeng was Hai Saeng. It wasn't like the change of place would make him less of himself, and it wasn't like you could control him as you please once he had opened up to you—he would only do what he wanted, fully aware of how to conduct himself. I imagined Hai Saeng dressed up in all-black, sitting underneath the bar's garish yellow light, playing a melancholic piano song that slowly turned into a tempest, his feet clad in leather shoes on a pedal, his head bobbing, the strands of hair next to his ears caught in the air, his eyes a pair of deep ponds, his delicate hands dancing through piano keys, his being a mirage somewhere between a demon and a priest, a shadow and a reflection.

Or, when he held a cue in his right hand, his left placed on the table's sea green baize, his index finger digging into its surface, his thumb curling inward, aiming for that white ball to knock the coloured balls into the holes accurately. Of course, Hai Saeng knew which guest had a pocket full of money, and who would tip him if he pretended to lose the game. The customers would order beer and insist that he drink it, and he would only take small sips just so Uncle wouldn't notice, or perhaps down the whole glass to anger him. Uncle Hirun's hair would turn completely grey if he continued to raise this nephew of his until the boy graduated, or perhaps he would be rejuvenated once again when he became an elder, hanging up his suit in exchange for a bike helmet, and ride a big bike from north through south with his old pals, leaving the bar behind for his nephew to look after.

The future is beyond anyone's grasp. Unless we drop dead, we still have to grow up and grow old among thousands of possibilities.

I swept all the broken pieces scattered about that house into a black rubbish bag and brought them to the garbage dump one by one. For stuff that could still be of use, I gave them away to the chess uncle to load onto his truck and sell them off. As for stuff that didn't look too broken, I snuck them back to their old place. The September air was cool and damp, and I tried to get everything done before it rained. Hai Saeng's house was so empty it looked like a burglar had snuck in. It was then that I found how the wallpaper, in the absence of decorations, was such a lame pattern that it made you feel down just from looking at it alone.

'Pink walls, green window frames, black roof.'

Our small talk that day—our grandest house renovation plan.

'And, a lime yellow kitchen,' I muttered, a smile surfacing on my face. I caressed the iron accessory poking out from underneath my school uniform with the tip of my finger and a heart full of love, then I put on my shoes and left Hai Saeng's house, walking along the paved road to head back to my shabby room.

*'Did you check the mailbox in front of my house?'*

*'I did.'*

*'Did you like the present?'*

In that small mailbox, I found a small necklace made of stainless steel in the same shape as a chain collar for dogs, an iron, rectangular name tag with smooth edges hanging from it. There was no owner name etched into the tag—there was no need, as I knew that name by heart. Next to the necklace was a piece of paper with a message written with a permanent marker, a message I couldn't stop myself from smiling at whenever I laid my eyes on it: **'Remember our summers and wait for my return'.**

# Murder of Crows

Upon one sleepless night, I heard a murder of crows chattering. Their *caw, caw* drifted all the way from the grove behind my house. Once I snuck in barefoote to spy on them and found them in the middle of a funeral. While the crow wearing a biretta was leading others in prayer, a young male crow leapt from the top of a pole to join them just in time.

'Here at last, here at last?' one of them cried.

'You're late, stupid,' another crow chimed in.

'I'm so sorry for coming late!' The crow that arrived late bobbed its head up and down. 'Is it time to eat, by the way?'

'Shh! Keep your voice down. Do you know manners? Manners. Do you know how to spell it?' the one in front screamed. Talk about the pot calling the kettle black— its voice was no less loud. Still, there was no point in complaining. These snoopy black birds wouldn't know how to lower their volumes; no wonder their caws could be heard metres away, and no wonder many were annoyed by them to the point that some would pick up brooms to swat them with it. The ceremony leader pretended not to hear them chatting, and the prayer for the departed continued.

'Ah, does anyone know why he died, by the way?' Another crow lacking in manners spoke up.

'Shh . . .'

'But I wanna know.'

'Everyone does, but are we really going to discuss the cause of our peer's death right in front of his body just so?'

They looked at each other.

The answer was: of course. It's completely normal for crows to huddle around a corpse that was one of them to determine the cause of death in order to watch out for their natural predators. They're one of the few animal species that know how to express sadness and are much smarter than avians in general. To do them justice, it might not be much of a stretch to say that they are smarter than animals. Still, they weren't all that smart in my opinion.

'Look at him smiling—cheeky enough to smile in death. He probably just stopped breathing and dropped dead, no?'

'Or perhaps he ate something bad. This guy would eat anything—even a rotting dog.'

'But that goes for you too.'

'Shut up. Beggars can't be choosers.'

'Shh. Do you know how to spell manners?'

'I don't.'

'Ca-caw!'

'Stop fighting.' A young, gossipy female crow squeezed in to join with the group, spreading her wings out to stop the fight. 'This isn't the time to be fighting among ourselves. I heard that he was killed.'

'Killed!' the crows gasped in surprise. 'Our friend was killed?!'

'But . . .'

'Shh!'

The prayer came to an abrupt end, with none of them able to focus any more after the taboo word *'killed'* was said. Their peer was killed, the crows discussed, having never heard that the deceased crow ever fought any other crows for females or trespassed into another's domain; it was never a threat and was rather stupider than most—every crow pitied it while looking to take advantage of it at the same time. The ceremony leader waited for the unproductive argument to slowly die down, then announced that an air show to honour the dead was up next.

'What? Is it not mealtime yet?' the most tardy one protested.

'Not yet,' every crow replied.

'Ahem,' the ceremony leader cleared his throat. 'Everyone, get in line. Is there anyone who is not ready?'

A voice mumbled from among the line that it needed to take a leak, but no crow paid it any mind. The ceremony leader walked to the front, then cried for the crows to start soaring—there was the second one, then the third one flapped its wings, soaring upward one after the other. They weren't as synchronized at first, unable to grasp the air currents just yet, not to mention how they weren't even flapping their wings in the same rhythm, and each turn they took was so crooked it was comical. However, not long after, their flight pattern finally fell into place: it was a ring, an eternal ring—the symbol of immortal life and one's eternal imprint on the hearts of their peers.

Still, as touching as the show was, I, having been crouching and spying on them for a while, could feel my muscles start to ache. The crows had already departed and left their dead peer behind in the clearing, so I crawled out of my hiding spot and inched closer to inspect the body. I nudged the wings that pressed close to the body away with my paw, revealing a deep wound and a most gruesome body, reeking of blood and drawing ants and flies in by the minute; it would soon become a feast. Poor thing.

The sound of wings piercing through the wind could be heard as it headed my way. I stepped aside just in time.

'A cat!' one of the crows screamed.

'Why is a cat here?!' another crow chimed in.

I slowly turned towards the source of the sounds. The crows landed on the ground one after the other and surrounded me in a circle, looking all haughty. The ceremony leader with a hat took a step forward and asked, 'What is a cat doing in a funeral for crows?'

'I just want to pay my respects to the deceased,' I feigned humility as I bowed my head down.

*Liar, liar.* The crows looked at each other, covering their beaks with their wings as they whispered.

'Didn't it come to eat the body?' a young female crow said.

'I think,' another young female crow added, 'this cat is the one who murdered our friend.'

I listened to them and laughed, then proceeded to ask, 'If I knew who killed your friend, would you avenge your friend?'

The whole lot of them looked at one another and mumbled, 'Of course.'

'Do you all swear?'

'Of course,' they replied.

'Do you all swear on your lives?' I asked yet again.

'Of course!'

'Wait,' the ceremony leader interjected. 'We would only give our oath when the matter concerns God. There's no need for us to swear to cats; crooked cats are our natural enemy.'

They all agreed. 'Go away, shoo, shoo.' They cried *caw, caw*. They wouldn't stop cawing and began flapping their wings to shoo me away. If it was a one-on-one fight, there was no way I would back down, but there were a whole lot of them—I had no choice but to flee. I leapt into the woods and ran, ran, ran away from the funeral of the crows. Their jeers followed me even after I had run a long distance away.

That night, just before I headed back home, I snuck a peek at the ceremony once more. The murder of crows was swarming around the corpse of the friend they had vowed to avenge, their heads bobbing up and down as they pecked at the dead body of their own kin, enjoying their midnight meal. It was as I thought—the grievous wounds I had seen on that body didn't belong to fangs and claws of four-legged predators like dogs and cats. They were, instead, left behind by the sharp, scissor-like beaks of crows.

The next morning, I told my friend the story. My wise, old calico stray friend yawned when I finished the story.

'And what is wrong with that?' the calico asked.

'Of course it is, they killed and ate their own kind—don't you find it strange?'

'You must have spent too much time with humans.' The calico purred in its throat in lieu of laughing. 'When it comes to the rule that one should never eat and harm their own kind, was it not humans alone who penned it?'

## Your Room

I unlock the door to your room and let myself fall onto your bed. Most of the stuff was left exactly how they were.

Hmm . . . The blanket with a seal pattern has your scent still. It's this funky, rank smell—I'm not saying that it smells bad—it's how you would expect young children's favourite, tattered blankets to smell like. How should I explain this? They said that young children would be attached to their favourite blankets and plush toys and have these articles clutched to their chest at all times, as these childhood blankets ward against harm, and children whose favourite blanket was destroyed by their parents would grow up to be sceptical of the world. You must have once curled up underneath this blanket on those days when the world gave you lemons, didn't you?

You left so many traces of you within this room that I have no idea how to remain breathing in it without your name slipping through my lips.

In the drawers, accessories and small trinkets are shoved together, all jumbled, never once organized—a trait you were born with. You barely brought anything to school at all, always paying for a new pen whenever you forgot your old one. Sometimes, you even took pens

133

that someone else had *left behind* on their desk as your own.

And when you said, '*they left it behind*', it meant that the other party only looked away for the briefest moment; you had nimble fingers and a kleptomaniac nature. Of course, all that was because you were too shy to ask anyone to borrow their stuff but had a mind bold enough to steal and remain unstirred even when cornered about your doing.

Regardless, what right do I have to judge you?

You haven't been around for long, but still, strands of your hair are left scattered on the floor of your room like weeds crawling atop the ground. They clumped up into a large seaweed-like ball at the drain in your bathroom. You refused to clean it up—you'd rather die than pick up disgusting stuff your body shed all around the room.

Coarse, curly black hair. You were envious of women who had long and silky black hair. You were so envious of them you couldn't hold it in.

I was there when it happened, when a large group of people were standing around you, their fingers pointed at you, accusing, '*She cut my hair. It was her.*'

You stood still, a pair of silver tailor's scissors in your hand, your gaze on them cold and silent, like a laser beam that pierced through everything. You didn't smile, didn't laugh, didn't cry, nor showed any sign of fear or distress; you simply stood there, wordless.

You didn't make any excuses. You had no proof, neither did those who accused you—but of course you did it. In this society that we grew up in, the majority rules above all; when they decided that you did it, then of course, it was you.

I looked around your room—a fifteen-square-metre space that once belonged completely to you. It's still hard to believe that I'll be living here from now on. You sent me the key and keycard to the room through the mail with a hastily drawn map. *The room's free to move in starting next month—I already told my family,*' you wrote in that letter.

Did you really tell your family? Your mom was shocked when I called her to let her know that I was moving in, and your dad was so furious he called me names through the phone. I had to take a photo of your letter and send it to them before they quieted down. No, they weren't unhappy with the proof nor too moved to pester me—I reckoned they were only at a loss for words.

Did you not hire anyone to clean up your room when you moved out? No wonder everything apart from your body and those tools were left the same—the electrical outlet that had a black burn mark from a faulty extension cord you bought from a 20-THB shop, and the microwave oven that once exploded when you put a stainless steel bowl inside instead of a glass bowl.

You had long been this way, no? *Clumsy*, I mean. There were many times I wondered if your clumsy nature was another one of your lies that you spewed as easily as greetings. You were always somehow injured or sick— having your arm in a cast just when we were about to have a P.E. test, or having a stomach ache so bad that you would have to lay down in the infirmary every Monday when we had the home economics class that you hated. You suddenly had an asthma attack when your classmate told you they had something to talk to you about, then you had an accident and had to be in a wheelchair for the rest of the semester when a sports festival was going on.

You always survived through your lies. All those accidents were carefully calculated—you simply had never succeeded with that thing before.

The OPP tape they tried so hard to scrape off left glue residue on the wall still. The smell of the gas was stuck in each furnishing piece.

I sat on your bed again, imagining how it must have happened.

You lay on this bed with a bottle of liquor and snacks that you liked, and there was this medicine in a brown bottle that you always had on you. It was during the day, I was certain. You hated the night, so you must have chosen daytime. You laid yourself down in your best clothes. You told yourself that you were certain, that you were going to be so happy. Your consciousness slowly melted away in the scorching sun at two in the afternoon. Your eyelashes slowly lowered down along with your eyelids. Still, believing as you might that you would be happy, you pressed your face into your blanket and wept.

While drawing in your last breath.

# Hide-and-Seek

## 1

My brother was honest to a fault. His best friend wasn't any better either. They were in the sixth grade, while I was in the third grade. We grew up neglected in a karaoke parlour in one cranny of the city. Dad was always drunk, as expected of a fun-loving man. Thankfully, his mood only got better when he drank, unlike ill-tempered drinking dads from other households. Mom didn't stay at home much, with a lot on her hands; for example, attending ballroom dances and meeting up with her sharing circles. Her employees were the only ones who stayed around to take a pity on us and bring us food, one meal after the other. Still, these ladies couldn't stay for long before they had to leave the parlour to marry whichever guest that got them pregnant, so we had to look after ourselves.

I realized that my ever-caring older brother had been spending less time with me ever since his sixth grade started. He had began telling me, 'You go home on your own today,' as soon as he parked his motorbike in the lot behind the school.

'Where are you going?' I asked.

'Is that your business?' he asked right back.

He bragged about how he had been on his own ever since first grade, and that I was already in third grade, so I should be able to find things to do on my own and not follow him around all day like a dog. His sneer was meant to send me packing, but it only added fuel to my curiosity and I began snooping around. I spied on him as he ran from class 6/5—his—to class 6/1 to greet his new friend. I heard that the guy had just moved to our school some weeks ago, was a swimmer, taller than kids his age, and pretty popular. How in the world did he become friends with someone so boring that plain water was flavourful in comparison—like my brother?

It was around this time that he began leaving me behind to go to school on my own while he rode away on his motorbike at dawn—probably visiting that friend before going to school together—and came back home late in the afternoon. *That's worrisome*, I thought, even with no one in this entire world caring about him at all. There was this one day when I intentionally let his new friend's name slip at the dining table with all our family members in attendance (which was a rare occasion). My brother was so taken aback that he choked on his soup.

'How did you know about that?!' he cried at the top of his lungs, all his cool lost, extremely suspicious to boot.

'How wouldn't I, let's ask that instead.' I rested my chin on my elbow.

'Who? Who is it?' Dad asked drowsily.

'It's nothing,' my brother interjected.

'His new friend,' I answered.

'Wow, our son has a friend?' Dad clicked his tongue.

'Is he rich?' Mom leaned in closer to join the conversation, invested.

'He's not!' he replied while glaring at me angrily. I feigned some tears; he got a friend and forgot about his younger brother, I told Mom, he doesn't love me, doesn't care about me any more.

I knew that he didn't want to introduce me to his new friend, but Mom made him after that evening.

'You're older, so you have to take care of your brother.' With that, Mom headed out for a round of evening Hi-Lo with Granny Iam.

'You have to listen to what your mom says, okay?' Dad said, yawning, then walked away to sing karaoke songs with a customer. They didn't really care if my brother would bring me with him as told, but he was a good kid who grew up listening to his parents, so there was no other choice for him but bringing me along when he went to meet up with his friend.

He said that his friend (to prevent further confusion, I'll call this friend of his Mr A from now on) was super cool, skilled mentally and physically, popular among teachers, and mixed-race to boot. My brother said that I needed to keep my mouth shut and say no nonsense around them. Judging from his fidgety looks, I was certain that my brother was totally charmed by this Mr A and was super afraid that he would be thrown aside, what with him being just a mediocre person who wasn't good at anything. I crossed my arms and laughed, then gave him a nod; whatever he said—I would go along with it all just to meet Mr A.

## 2

Mr A's family owned an internet café. 'It belongs to *Gu*,' Mr A referred to his mother's brother with a Teochew term. 'Gu Aew,' we greeted Gu Aew, the owner of the internet café. He was a middle-aged man with a beer belly who was always kind to children—if Gu Aew would ever wear red from head to toe, I was sure that I would unknowingly call him Santa Claus. Mr A told us that his mother had just recently been put in jail for having fatally shot her *farang* husband when drunk.

'One of them had a gun, another a foul mouth. They had been at each other's throats for a decade, I wonder why they only managed to actually do it now,' Mr A said without a care. My brother found Mr A's nonchalence extremely cool, while I found the guy odd.

And of course he was odd—I found that out just a bit later when we were playing together. Mr A and I would join hands in cheating on my brother in any games we played without giving any signals whatsoever to each other. He would distract my brother while he was playing Street Fighter against me, prodding him to give answers to Mr A's witty questions while I smashed away at the buttons.

'Answer me now, my dear friend. How many provinces does Bangkok have?'

'Huh? Of course it's seventy-six,' he answered right away.

'Are you sure? Think about it,' Mr A drawled, then we both burst out laughing.

Mr A and I became accomplices in every single game: draughts, Old Maid, and even the games of tag and hide-and-seek we played in the city pillar shrine. He once helped me to slip into an underground storage drawer. My brother could only find my shoes. He yelled, threatening and calling me names to show up until the sun went down without a single sighting of me. Mr A coaxed him to head home, while Dad and Mom did not, even once, ask after me. I slipped in and out of that drawer, sneaking around shrine caretakers with Mr A bringing me food for three whole days.

'How's Brother?' I asked.

'Cried like a baby,' Mr A answered. 'He kept pacing around, talking about reporting to the police. I told him that if his parents knew he had lost his younger brother, he'd be the one in trouble. Now we don't get to play PES together at all—his only concern is running around the market looking for you.'

'I see, I see.' I nodded, quite happy about my importance to my brother.

'And what about you?'

'I'm all sore,' I answered. 'The food isn't good either.'

'Are you not afraid of ghosts?'

'They aren't even real.'

'What a boring kid you are.' Mr A chuckled. 'All right, let's go back today.'

He held his hand out to me and helped me get up. When my feet first touched the scorching concrete floor and my skin got to taste the sun, I staggered to the side, feeling as if my body couldn't remember its previous ordinary days. Mr A took hold of my shoulder, and when I found my footing, he gently pushed it.

'You're a weird kid,' Mr A commented.

I didn't answer. He was much taller than me, that much was true, but he was also another kid just like me. We walked through alleys bathed in the heat of sunlight at dusk, treading underneath a bridge. The river glimmered like golden satin from Middle Easterners' fabric shops. Some spotted me and nudged their friends. 'That's Jaa's son that went missing.' 'He's doing fine, isn't he,' their friends answered. With that, they no longer paid us any mind.

Once Dad's karaoke parlour came into view, my brother ran out of the door to meet us.

'I reckon I should tell you this,' Mr A softly whispered while my brother was still on his way towards us. 'I only realized this when you went missing. I actually like it when that guy cries.'

'That's no secret.' I narrowed my eyes.

'Is it that obvious?'

'I could see it all the way from the moon.'

Brother reached us and pulled me into a hug, his tears staining my shirt. Question after question poured forth from his mouth; for example, where was I, was I doing okay, was I hurt anywhere, how did I find my way back, and how did Mr A find me. I replied to none of them and only proceeded to pat his back gently while glancing over at Mr A, who was smiling sweetly as if he was watching some heartwarming family movie.

You psycho—the words surfaced in my mind, but I didn't say them out loud.

Whatever. I understood him, actually, as I also had secrets of my own.

## 3

The older brother's pair of arms that held me in a tight hug was damp with tears, staining the shirt with wet circles. I buried my face in his shirt for a while, and it was then that old memories resurfaced.

Have I ever told you guys about how my parents never held me, as far back as my memory takes me? My brother told me that they were fawning over him before I was born, kissing his baby cheeks and hugging him close like a pair of newlyweds would do. They wanted to have him; he was in their family plan. I, on the other hand, wasn't. I was an accident from not pulling out in time— as for what 'not pulling out in time' was, Brother didn't elaborate.

'That's not the truth, though. You were actually born in a bin,' my brother said jokingly.

I could hear it from his tone of voice that he was just joking, but I had been thinking more about that lately. Parents who provided you with a house to sleep in, paid for your tuition fees, never hit you but didn't care much for you either, letting you grow up on your own—*Being rubbish's child wouldn't be too bad*, would it? I thought as I crawled to sleep in a bin.

I buried my face in my knees and used a rubbish bag as a makeshift pillow. There was not much space left for a kindergartner to curl up, but it was safe. It was as if a dozen gentle, warm hands were reaching out towards me, caressing me with the touches my parents had deprived me of during my infant years. Narrow spaces made me feel safe, embracing me like a mother's womb.

Next morning, a female employee from the karaoke parlour screamed at the top of her lungs when she opened the bin to find me suckling on my thumb like a baby in a womb. I explained to my parents why I had decided to sleep in there. They hurriedly explained to me that it wasn't so, that I was really their child and that they loved me to death. Still, no one leapt out to hug me—probably due to how bad I smelled.

I couldn't remember how many more times I climbed to sleep in a bin again during that short period of my life. My parents got used to it. They stopped pampering me and chose to scare me instead with a story of how ghosts would spirit me away if I went outside at night. After that, I stopped climbing into bins. They thought that it must be due to that ghost story.

'Are you not afraid of ghosts?'

'They aren't even real.'

This world doesn't have ghosts. That much I know. I have long been searching for proof of this.

What exist are ants, termites, cockroaches, sewer rats, and house lizards. They're everywhere—wardrobe drawers, spaces in gutters, and cracks in walls. No matter how clean your room is, they are still living in secret behind the facade, marching in lines, eating away at your tiny home ever so quietly until it comes tumbling down.

My secret was, I loved shoving myself into these narrow spaces. I knew how to contort my body, dislocate my joints, fold my arms and legs—the smaller I folded them, the better. On sleepless nights after

I was forbidden from sleeping in the bin, I would hide away in corners of the karaoke rooms, watching live the interactions between our customers and young female employees. I spent some nights in a cranny between buildings, observing as policemen rode their motorbikes to get their share of bribe money from Dad after a trip to sneak some drugs into the possession of clueless biker boys a street over. All of this took place when my brother believed that I was still sleeping in the top bunk bed. I was never once caught—Brother was so daft, how could he know anything?

## 4

'Say, what's the narrowest space you've ever squeezed yourself in to?' Mr A asked. I kicked my feet in the air for a while, thinking, then I answered, 'A traffic cone.'

'Holy shit.'

'I was younger, so I managed to.'

'Did your head not get stuck?'

'Scrunch down your neck, that's how.'

I told him of my mission where I had made my way from the entrance of a market to its back, eighteen metres in total, inching forward underneath a traffic cone.

'Did no one see you moving at all?'

'Wanna try?'

I showed it to him. However, as I was too big to fit into a traffic cone, we opted for the leaves basket of a street sweeper instead. I told him that I would make my way around King Rama IV Monument in front of Khao Wang in six hours, which Mr A agreed to sit and watch. This test ended within two hours because of the street sweeper uncle, the owner of that basket, who walked around the area looking for it. We ended up getting scolded by him for our mischievous game.

Our games didn't stop at that.

Saturday afternoon, I was riding in the backseat of my brother's motorbike, heading for Chao Samran beach. Mr A was riding another motorbike next to us. The three of us swam around until each of our skin was scorched several shades darker. Once the sun began to set, we laid ourselves on the sandy beach to dry. Mr A gave my brother some money to buy dried squid and crispy roti from a pushcart next to the beach. Once Brother was out of our sight, he turned to me. I looked back at him, fully aware that he was about to propose some crazy scheme again.

We had taken turns digging a hole on the beach prior to that. Once my brother was away, I got in that hole and had Mr A cover my body with sand up to my chin. We had to be quick with it. Mr A used his feet to level the area above the hole to match the surrounding sandy areas, then hurriedly put a basket around my head. Once Brother came back, he no longer saw me.

'Where's my brother?' he asked.

'I don't see him anywhere—probably drowned to death already,' Mr A answered.

'Be serious.'

'Are you a nursing mom? The kid's probably just playing around here.'

Mr A patted the sandy ground next to him, telling my brother to sit down and snack together, which Brother only did because he wanted to look cool in his friend's eyes. Still, he couldn't keep cool for long before he started fidgeting around—an act which didn't escape the eyes of his friend in the least.

'What are you looking for, my dear friend?'

'My brother isn't back yet,' he replied with a shaky voice.

Mr A pointed at a single sandal floating in the sea. It was mine—I had no idea when exactly he had thrown it away.

'Is that your brother's?'

My brother's face went pale in that instant. He ran into the sea, calling my name. Everyone in the vicinity looked at him. I, seeing the world through evenly spaced holes, had to try my darndest to not laugh and make cracks in the sand.

Mr A leaned closer to me, whispering softly, 'How do you feel?'

'So good, it feels as if I'm a seed,' I replied.

I really felt that way. The dry sand was warm, and the wet sand was cool on my skin. I wanted to fall asleep right there so I could wake up as a beachside flower.

'What a weird one,' Mr A muttered and continued, 'If I leave you here, for how many days do you reckon you can remain like this? Was three days from the last time your limit?'

'Three days was nothing.'

I told Mr A about a book I once read. In the US, there was a trespasser who snuck inside a gap between the walls on the second floor of an old couple's house for nine months. He only intended to take a brief respite from the cold wind at first, but then he found the place comfortable and stayed long-term. One day, the house owner found him, so the guy accidentally killed the house owner. This turned into a huge investigation. Still, before the guy was caught, he slipped back into the gap and remained hidden for months.

'There's no need to go to that extent.' Mr A laughed and took the basket off my head. 'Well, your brother's losing his mind. It's time you get out.'

I freed myself from the sand and crawled back up to sit with my legs crossed as if nothing had happened at all. While I got up to brush sand off myself, Mr A put a hand next to his mouth and shouted for my brother to turn around.

Of course, Brother was so mad, but he was crying at the same time—he wasn't good at keeping his emotions inside. In spite of his curses that shortly followed, completely directed at us, knowing his true heart in that short span of time made me happy from feeling needed.

To say that Brother's tears were like hands that stretched out towards me, a single pair of hands that roped me back to reality, wouldn't be much of a stretch.

## 5

When I started fourth grade, my brother and his friend got into the provincial high school together. Mr A grew as tall as a bamboo tree with Brother following close behind at ten centimetres shorter. They took turns rubbing my head, telling me to drink a lot of milk to catch up to them quickly.

Another one of my secrets: I poured my milk into a dog's bowl behind everyone's back—I didn't want to grow up, you see.

## 6

I didn't want to grow up, but this damned body kept getting taller every year. I used my brother's hand-me-down school uniforms, which a young female employee at the parlour removed my brother's embroidered name from and replaced with mine. Mom muttered that I was growing at a much faster pace than my brother, and it wouldn't be long before I couldn't wear his clothes. Her tone of voice wasn't too happy. Dad, on the other hand, only yawned when he heard her grumbling and said: isn't it good that our son grows up quickly so he would be tall?

I agreed with Mom on this matter. Be it crannies between walls, bins, or even baskets intended for fallen leaves, I used to be able to fit in all of them. I was growing up so quickly that I was unhappy with it myself.

From hands in the darkness that once caressed and embraced me as one of their own, they slowly turned into a suffocating space, into shunning shoves. Leave, get out, you're an adult already, said the ants and insects, don't take up our spaces.

Even the womb of my actual mother can't care for me forever, can it? I thought forlornly as I sat hugging my knees in front of the drawer in the shrine that I once hid inside. After a long while, I saw the tall shadow of Mr A next to mine.

I said without looking at him, 'I have something I want to trouble you with. If it's you, you'll certainly do it for me.'

'I will?' Mr A replied. 'If I do, what would I get in return?'

'Anything. What do you want?'

'Can I have your brother?'

'Sure.'

'Hey, I'm being serious here.'

'Of course I am being serious.'

Mr A rested his chin on his elbow, intrigued. But once I revealed what I wanted his help with, he took a step back, exclaiming, 'You're out of your mind!'

My request was: have him cement me into the wall.

'You aren't gonna do it?'

'Damn, damn, damn—anyone who agrees would be out of their mind. Have you ever thought about what would happen if the adults found out about that?'

'Don't let them, then.' I flopped on to the ground and rolled around. 'Just like always.'

'No, kiddo, this is *nothing* like always.'

Mr A was dead set on his refusal. It was the first time I ever saw him being so adamant about something.

*Mr A has changed*, I thought. He began saying '*no*' to me instead of '*sure, let's give it a try*'. I noticed that his eyes weren't as crystal clear as when we first met, and he sometimes walked with hunched shoulders, as if he was embarrassed of his height. His flawless face, too, had red pimples appearing here and there. He was about to grow up into a boring adult—so was my hunch.

Mr A must have noticed that I went quiet for a long moment, because he looked down at me. Then, his face went pale; his lips frowned like someone in shock and an extreme amount of pain. He looked away from me right that instant.

What did he see? My guess was that he saw his own reflection bathed in disappointment in a fourth-grader's eyes—a fourth grader who played with him like his own little brother, a fourth grader who had long respected him as his accomplice.

He couldn't stand it.

Both of us remained silent until the sun was about to set behind the horizon. Mr A was the first to get up. He reached his hand out to pull me back up on my feet. We walked back home in silence.

I remember him calling the parlour that night. A female employee woke me up to talk to him.

'Let's give it a try—this thing that you asked.' I heard him speaking quietly through the phone. 'But we can't rush it, if that's all right with you?'


## 7


Having listened to my story up to this point, you must be imagining that Mr A would come to spend time with me from then on instead of being with my older brother, and the poor guy would be left behind on his own, oblivious to everything. That, however, wasn't the case. Mr A was still spending time with Brother like always; I was the one who disappeared.

Or to be precise, Mr A made me disappear.

Wherever it may be that he met up with my brother, Mr A would look for nooks and crannies where he could shove me in between. He ever so patiently positioned me into the space so that I could observe him and my brother as they studied for exams, discussed obscene topics that they wouldn't mention with me around, or talked about a girl—one of the upperclassmen—that my brother had a crush on. When it was time for them to say goodbye, Mr A would wait for my brother to leave first, then bend down to ask me, 'How is it? Is this place good?'

I pondered and shook my head. It was all right, but, no, it was not the place.

Mr A sighed as if relieved. 'There's no need to rush. You have to make a careful choice, since you'll stay there forever,' he said. We moved from one place to another after that. Mr A would settle for answers such as, 'This is all right,' or 'I'll come to like it'. He said that I shouldn't be so sloppy with the plan, but I believed that he was only buying time.

I had no right to blame him, of course. I knew that I was buying time myself too.

But I just didn't want to grow up.


## 8

Like thunder in broad daylight, my brother proudly announced at the dining table one evening, 'I have a girlfriend now.'

'Whoa,' Dad exclaimed. 'So, our son does have a girlfriend. Who is it? Who?'

'Phee Pan, she's my senior from eighth grade,' he answered. 'She does traditional dance too—very cute.'

'Is she rich?' my mom chimed in. Her question was totally ignored, but it was all right—she would snoop around until she found out about the girl's great-great grandparents by tomorrow.

'What about Mr A?' I asked.

He was confused. 'What does Mr A have to do with this?'

Mr A likes you, doesn't he? That was the question I was too reluctant to ask, afraid that I would ruin whatever they had, so I asked Mr A behind Brother's back.

'It isn't like you to let your prey wriggle away like this,' I said. Mr A shrugged, nonchalant, but I could notice that he was somewhat irritated.

With my brother now having a girlfriend, the relationship between us three underwent small changes. You see, ever since the first day my brother had gotten to know Mr A, I had long thought that my brother would be dumped in the blink of an eye, but that wasn't the case. The outstanding Mr A deigned to grace us with roughly a year of his companionship, while Brother was the one to disappear first. He would be busy taking his girlfriend out to have ice cream, or maybe enjoy movies with just the two of them—all of which left Mr A disoriented. He never mentioned the thing that the two of us agreed to do any more. Without my brother, all our activities came to a halt. We spent time together half-heartedly, swimming, playing badminton, or playing computer games at Gu Aew's internet café just to while away the time.

Brother returned to us within two months, dumped by the girl.

'Girls are so fucking heartless!' he cried, hugging his knees close to his chest. 'Give me music!'

Mr A was playing guitar next to him, providing him with emotional background music. '*It's a farewell party, saying goodbye to this aching pain and gut-wrenching sadness! It's a farewell party, wishing you and him a long-lasting love!*'

I sang with him, '*Best of luck to you, leaving behind this man that you don't yearn for.*'

My brother soloed the last line of lyrics, '*Get me the bill, I'll pay for this whole sadness that I asked for.*'

'Boo, you're now single again, booooo,' Mr A poked fun at him with booing.

'Booooo, no one wants you!' I giggled along.

At first, Brother wasn't too happy that we seemed to be so satisfied by the fact that he was dumped, but who could remain angry at Mr A for long? With his personality, he successfully convinced my brother within a few minutes that youth is better spent on friendship rather than love.

Regardless, my brother had a new girlfriend by next week—an older girl from the school library who would break up with him within the next three months. Then, he would go on to woo the enthusiastic class vice president, who would dump him to secretly date the teacher who taught ethics. This would turn out to be perfect timing for a volleyball athlete from tenth grade who adored my brother's stubby hair and beady polar-bear-like eyes to come in and mend his broken heart. She would then ask him to attend the Loy Krathong festival together, which he would agree to and would leave us all by ourselves again.

Every single time that Brother had a girlfriend, Mr A would get increasingly annoyed. This emotional turbulence would calm down somewhat when my brother returned with a broken heart, but it never completely disappeared. I had no idea what was on his mind that night either—he might have wanted an outlet for his obsession over my brother, or simply remembered our promise.

'Let's do it, this thing that you asked of me,' Mr A told me on a phone call. 'I think I'm ready.'

## 9

'He'll show up before long.'

'Huh, don't you want to go look for him together?'

'How long do you think I'll keep falling for you guys' pranks? I'm not stupid.'

Mr A told me that my brother said so when he tried asking about me.

I had been crouching in a corner of a building which was one part of an abandoned swimming pool for three days now. Mr A hadn't gotten around to cementing me into the building just yet. He said that he had to wait; he had to wait for something to happen, perhaps for the constellations in the sky to make their journeys, for stars to line up, or just for Brother to say something that he himself would later regret.

*He'll show up before long.*

He laughed alone like a madman. 'You brother thought that you'd return to him. If only he knew he made a mistake, what kind of face would he make? Would he cry? I'm having so much fun with my imagination alone.'

With that, Mr A threw me a bottle of cheap drinking water and a pork floss with bologna sandwich.

'Eat that,' he said. 'We'll begin once you're full.'

'I'll die soon—there's no need to eat,' I objected.

'Even death row inmates can have their last supper, so what kind of a heartless bastard do you think I am that won't let you have one?'

'But death row inmates can choose their meal.'

'And now we're being picky.'

We both laughed. Then, a frightening silence took over the area surrounding us.

Mr A began mixing the cement: sand and cement first, followed by water and crushed stones. He didn't look too elegant in the process, having never done it before. He had to ask the grown-ups and learn by observing at construction sites, and staying too long at the place was out of question, or they would find him suspicious (since he's a tall teen with a farang-looking face, you only need to see him once to remember him forever). I was grateful for his dedication to my cause, but I was a bit hurt at the same time, for his motivation wholly revolved around my brother alone.

He finished mixing the cement, looked at me, then swore quietly under his breath. I asked if something was wrong. He didn't answer, and only pulled me out of the small crack that I had been staying inside for three days by my arm, then dragged me along until we reached a suffocatingly small room that must have once been a changing closet. He pushed me down on to the ground, then began laying bricks at its threshold.

'What does this mean?' I cried as I got up, but I was pushed down again.

Why was he changing the spot? I asked again. This wasn't our agreed method of making me part of a wall—I should be crouching and unable to move at all, shouldn't I? Why did Mr A change his mind all of a sudden? What was he thinking? Was he going to betray me?

I got up and was about to step across the brick wall that didn't come up to my knee just yet. Seeing that, Mr A got up and punched my face, taking me by surprise. When he saw me resisting, he punched me again in my stomach.

'Stay here, don't act up.' Mr A's voice was shaking. I suspected that he was crying.

I could taste bitter blood and bile rising up my throat, accompanied by a stinging pain in my stomach that had me slumping to the ground. I clutched my stomach, crying, asking him to explain, to tell me why wasn't he doing what I had asked him to—why was he doing this? What was he planning to do afterward? Mr A, however, refused to say anything until the last brick was placed, blocking all light from me.

## 10

My hands and feet began to feel numb. I was running out of air. It felt as if only a few seconds had passed and simultaneously felt an eternity. The sun must have risen, and perhaps set too. I might have long run out of air, which would explain my indifference towards everything.

It was only painful when he punched me, which turned into numbness after a short moment. I thought it would be suffocating, but I didn't feel so at all. I wasn't even hungry. I felt so light, save for the smell which was a bit too musty. While the place was too dark for me to see my surroundings, the room that was larger than me to begin with only felt more spacious. Was my body shrinking down?

If so, that would be awesome. I would continue to shrink down, from a ten-year-old to a nine-year-old, then keep getting smaller until I reach the size of a three-year-old, a two-year-old, and finally turn into a lump of flesh in a mother's belly. A baby in the womb. The womb of rubbish.

That gentle hand was back again. It stretched towards me, touched my head, consoled me, and cared for me in the way that my parents never did. I slept in a soft lap, listening to a lullaby. I could hear my brother's crying in that singing voice. My brother who once wept because he couldn't find me—he was there. And Mr A was playing a guitar next to him, laughing along.

Is this the truth? Is this merely a dream of a child nearing his death? I asked.

'A dream, of course,' Mr A answered, 'as he's still unable to find you even now.'

Mr A said thus and walked around me, crouching on the floor like a cocoon. I looked up at him. He seemed much younger than when I last met him—turned back into a gleeful sixth grader.

'Whenever we talked about you, he would cry.' Mr A met my gaze. He smiled and continued in no hurry. 'Year after year, he only blamed himself for not having headed out and looked for you. He blamed himself for having a girlfriend. This matter concerning you turned into his lifelong regret—cool, isn't it? I adore your brother's crying face the most.'

Mr A laughed. Seeing me quiet, his smile faded.

'Hey, do you regret it?' he asked.

*Regret what?* I thought, but didn't ask back.

'Everything.'

*I don't know. I don't know what I want either.*

Once I told him that, Mr A's brows furrowed.

He opened his mouth as if he wanted to say something, but this visage of him was washed away by the blinding white light that came pouring forth in the blink of an eye.

*Bam!*

*Bam!*

'The boy's stuck here!'

'I repeat, we found the boy!'

'He's alive!'

## 11

My memory concerning the event was muddled at best. I'll try my best going through the whole thing.

They found me, dehydrated, with hypoxia, and the most worrisome inability to articulate words. I was sent to the hospital. My brother cried, having found me at last. He had help from the adults in the area and many policemen, each of them looking at places of interest, based on information provided by the folks that once saw me walking away with Mr A.

Fortunately, Mr A's brick wall wasn't too sturdy; it came tumbling down with a hammer and chisel. Folks in the community were shocked by the news, and it eventually reached my mother's ears as she was losing hard in a Hi-Lo game, followed by my dad who was drunk out of his mind, flanked by karaoke parlour ladies. They were called in by the police for child negligence and came back fawning over me for a while before everything returned to normal.

As for Mr A, Brother said that Mr A appeared at the karaoke parlour's ground floor after trapping me inside the room, throwing a small stone at his window. Once their eyes met, Mr A waved goodbye. When Brother ran downstairs to meet him, he had disappeared. No one had seen him ever since. My parents and my brother reported to the police that Mr A was the perpetrator. They asked me for a confirmation of the culprit's identity, but I kept quiet, refusing to answer any question. They concluded that I was suffering from emotional distress to the point that I was unable to provide any useful information for the case.

My brother, however, knew that I had lied. He was the only person I talked about the incident with.

I told him that I never thought he would locate me, and that I was sorry for having long thought that he was dumb.

'Yeah, I'm dumb, but not that dumb. Do you now understand?' he replied. I thought that he was so cool at that moment, and how nice it was to stay alive.

## 12

Eight years later, I met Mr A accidentally at a Japanese restaurant in Bangkok. I was celebrating the end of freshmen-welcoming period with a dozen freshmen friends. When I glanced over at a cook as he was tossing a wok on the stovetop, my eyes stumbled upon a man with glasses who seemed to be enjoying his solitude, sitting alone at a table further away. He was pushing around a straw paper wrapper in a small puddle atop his table with a pair of chopsticks. I remembered him instantly; he, likewise. I raised my hand to greet him, to which he nodded and gestured towards the smoking area just outside of the restaurant.

'You're so much taller,' were the first words he said to me.

'And you're much older,' I replied.

Mr A told me that I wasn't cute any more—how dare I grow taller than both my brother and him.

I agreed. A small kid that had once fit himself in small crannies of an eighteen-metre market had taken his departure from this world, leaving behind the core of him wrapped in another's skin. I had become a boring adult; him, too. He changed the topic right away when I asked what he was doing, where was he working, or with whom.

'How's your brother?'

'He has just broken up with his girlfriend,' I told him, knowing full well that the question was just an act. 'Drunk at home right now, perhaps.'

'He never learns.'

'He attracts only awful people, that's why.'

'It feels as if I'm being called out.'

We looked at each other and laughed.

'Hey, A.'

'Hmm?'

I asked him the question I hadn't dared ask when I was young. 'Weren't you planning to confess your love to him at all?'

Mr A went quiet for so long it looked like he was stunned. Then, he shook his head rapidly and said, 'It has been so long already—I don't really remember how I felt back then any more.'

I said nothing else after that. None of us said anything.

Mr A scratched the back of his neck and said, 'You are angry at me, aren't you?'

I asked him what I was supposed to be angry about. For trapping me inside a room instead of cementing me into a wall as I asked. For doing things as he pleased, and even hurting me in the process.

'Don't think too much about it,' I said. 'I'm quite satisfied with how things turned out—how could I possibly be angry at you?'

Mr A bit his lower lip. 'I was just afraid.' He looked down, muttering, his hair covering his face. 'I wanted to teach your brother how it feels like to lose one dear to you, but when the time came, I chickened out. Back then,

I wondered how it was even possible to cement someone into a wall, not to mention a kid that I had spent so much time with—how could I possibly do it? But now, if I were to do that again, I might be able to. Yes, I think I can. What do you think?'

'Are you asking me to?' I laughed.

Mr A looked up at me. A considerate smile of an adult appeared on his face.

'No. I don't think I can,' Mr A said as he patted my back gently. 'You're already a grown-up, after all.'

That night, we bid each other goodbye. He returned to his table, and I returned to my group of freshmen friends. Our celebration lasted until half an hour before midnight. I headed back in the same direction as a couple of girls. The Skytrain's headlight bathed the platform in a yellowish-white hue.

'What's the frown for?' One of the girls jabbed me in the side with her elbow.

I laughed and blinked rapidly to erase Mr A's pitiful smile from my mind.

# Conch

Every time she presses her ear against a conch, she hears the sound of the sea—the sea next to which her grandmother once built a house. Her grandmother told her that she would walk along the beach in the morning, gazing at the sun as it rose behind the clouds, casting down its reflection on to the water's surface like a giant bolt of pink satin. The sea that was calm yet ferocious at the same time. The water surface that was cool and yet so warm once you dipped your feet in. The fishermen who lived by the sea in their hammocks would come back with their fishing nets just as the horse-keeper brought out his young, brown horse to look for the first customers of the day.

Her grandmother kept the sea in a conch shell. It was a murex shell with a natural hue of white and orange and long scratches on its surface. 'Listen to it,' her grandmother said to her when she was just a baby. The vast ocean contains thousands of stories: confessions of love-stricken ones, tears of those that got their hearts broken, and the last wishes of drowned sailors. Listen to it, lovers of different races meet each other in secret in a seaside cave. An alluring laugh, the sound of skin rubbing against one another, the sound of limbs wrapping together atop the sandy beach, the sound of droplets that fall down long, black hair, and whispers of love as they promise to meet each other again beneath a starry sky. When the lady's family finds out about her secret love, when the man waits for her alone, when the water rises up high without any sight of her, when her father's henchmen roll a boulder to block the cave entrance, and when the man drowns with a heart full of love and vengeance.

*Listen to it*, an offshore wind that carries a small boat towards the ocean. The onshore wind that brings squid boats back home. The sound of the waves that sound like a single note—no, perhaps a single chord that plays over and over in an even tempo, lulling one to sleep. '*How could the sea be calm and furious at the same time?*' she wondered. Her grandmother laughed. '*Just like humans,*' the old lady answered off-topic, '*just like women.*'

Listen to it, ladies of the ocean dance just beneath the water surface. Their blue skirts swirl in fine bubbles. Their eyes are emotionless. No one can steal from them any more, as they have nothing left. They are the souls of the women that were killed in rains amidst the ocean—women who were badly hurt, physically and mentally, women who lost everything they had in their possession, women who no longer wished to be found. They surf the wind like sailboats during stormy nights until they reach the boulders along the beach, upon which they sit combing each other's hair, singing songs that sound akin to hymns, but the actual lyrics are filled with the words of a curse.

*Listen to it.* She tried to imagine how her grandmother once talked gently to her, back when she was so young, back when her family were together, before her grandmother would die of old age, before her parents would divorce and send her away to grow up in the capital city. Before she would get married to a serious young man who knew not a single bedtime story, before they would have a child together—a child who loved swimming, yet never once visited the sea.

The seas in the area have long been unsuitable for swimming. She told her child thus during their drive to the provincial indoor swimming pool. The seas in the area have long been unsuitable for swimming ever since the oil spill that weighed nearly a hundred thousand ton muddied the ocean water. Many environmentalists from the newer generations were outspoken about their desire to solve this problem, but documents required by the bureaucratic procedures were delayed within the system itself, allowing the oil spill to first reach the shore and slaughter way too much of the marine ecosystem. Questions arose from the public, but they were all buried in the wake of celebrity drama.

The government spokesperson told us to remain calm, and that nature would certainly mend itself even if it needs a decade. 'The sea will be crystal clear again within that time span, and our province will become a tourist hotspot of Southeast Asia again.' This, however, was a big lie, just like other press releases that didn't hold any more weight than a whiff of fart. When that private sector company who let the oil spill didn't have to take any responsibility, it seemed to prompt other companies to let their chemical waste spill into the sea year in and year out. Local fisherman communities were no more, and tourism had no chance of resurfacing. The seas in the area had long been unsuitable for swimming. Its sight disturbed everyone. No one wanted to breathe in the air at a pungent black beach with toxic waste bobbing atop the water surface—no one wanted to bring their children to such a place. The provincial agency put up a barbed wire fence along the area, separating the people from the ocean and the fishermen from their own roots.

'But seas at other places are still good, right, mommy?' the girl asked.

Her mother smiled a melancholic smile. *Of course.* She was saving up, and when she had saved enough, she would take her daughter away, far away from her stern father, from this sad and dirty town, towards the south where the sea remained turquoise blue. She'll go there someday, she promised herself.

Since things weren't in her favour just yet, she could only give her daughter the conch as her grandmother once did. Press the conch close to your ear, then close your eyes. When you do that, you'll hear the sound of the sea.

# The Case of the Hair Trimmer

## 1

There existed at least one Ploy in every school—no, everywhere in this country.

Ploy Jah, Ploy Sai, Pretty Ploy, Sickly Ploy, Moody Ploy—Ploys were never left alone by those in their lives, give them one minute and they'll provide their Ploys with some kind of adjectives to their names. Sometimes their names will be made more international instead with Poito, Point, Paloy, Paula, and Paulie among many.

But I reckon no other Ploys within this school had a name worse than mine.

I was the Cockroach Ploy.

Everyone there hated me.

If you were to ask me when the girls began to hate me to this extent, I would answer that it must have originated from one small coincidence. I always had pens or pencils of the same brand as some classmates that had lost theirs. One of them would ask me, 'Did you buy this one or find it?'

'I bought it,' I would reply.

No one thought much of it at first, but when this kind of instance continued, my classmates began talking behind my back, saying I was a thief. Later on, their nosy gazes began to nitpick at my clothing. 'That comb must have been Ploy Jah's, and didn't Poito tell us that her red Evita hair clip went missing last week? Why's she using it?'

'She must have stolen them,' they concluded.

Why was I in the wrong? They never took notice of everyone in the school already having this kind of stuff in their possession; they had simply long been looking to accuse me.

I had a multitude of ways to weather all their malicious gossip—pretending like I heard nothing or that I was playing a survival game on an island full of crazy people, for instance. I never told my parents—a father and mother who worked tirelessly in another province most likely wouldn't be looking forward to news of how their daughter couldn't fit in with other students in a boarding school. As for the teachers, they distanced themselves from clashes between the kids (which I didn't blame them for—they must have had enough of interfering only to be hated by all parties in the end). I turned into an outcast among young girls of the same age, and I thought that I was at rock bottom already, only to find out that things could get worse. One afternoon when a teacher gave us something to work on as she headed out for a department meeting, Sickly Ploy pointedly scorned me with full intention for everyone in the craft workshop to hear.

'I paid a lot for that pair of scissors, what a bummer that some dog had to steal it to use as their own.' She looked up and yelled across the room. 'Are you so neglected by your family that you have to take others' stuff?'

I knew she meant the pair of red, half-worn scissors in my hand, an ordinary pair of scissors that half of my classmates had in their possession, as it was the kind that the school's supply store had for sale. Everyone continued to work on their tasks. No one took that crazy one's side and neither did anyone take my side. That was how we lived. As long as you weren't the target, you could look the other way and survive another day. However, I was quite annoyed on that day to begin with, so everyone in class M 3/2 got to see me standing up for myself for the first time, the sound of my hand hitting the table's surface echoing in the room.

'Who is it? Let's hear the name,' I shouted.

Sickly Ploy had a big mouth yet lacked courage. She agitatedly averted her eyes, completely taken by surprise that I, too, had a mouth to defend myself with.

'Yeah, I wanna know too. Who took your stuff? Say their name, come on,' I continued to talk in her face. She looked the other way at this point, the way her body shivered like a chihuahua was utterly pitiful in my eyes. Perhaps I became too smug when I leaned my face closer to hers and said through gritted teeth with a very audible voice for all to hear, 'If you won't leave me alone, I'll cut your fucking hair when you sleep tonight.'

I only intended to put her back in her place with a threat, which I, in essence, succeeded at.

Because I turned into a culprit within the following week.

They called the incident 'the case of the hair trimmer'.

## 2

For girls in junior high, hair was everything. It was more important than their brows, any accessories, or visits to dermatologists for their acne.

Hair on their nape that was meticulously thinned, bangs, side bangs, and loose threads of hair next to their ears—lower secondary schoolers aren't allowed to wear long hair, so great care is put in styling their short hair.

It happened on a night when all ninth graders had already gone to bed. To prevent further confusion, let me explain the overview of our dorm. Our boarding school had students from each year sleeping together—around a hundred students from the same year slept together in the same room with welded bunk beds and hard mattresses lined up side by side, leaving almost no space to walk around. At bedtime, students from the senior year on duty would take turns herding younger students upstairs.

Everyone was supposed to be in their bed by nine-thirty. Those on security duty would turn off the lights in their respective zones, dousing everything in darkness until five-thirty the next morning. Whatever that might take place during that time would happen in pitch-black ignorance.

The culprit took the opportunity to slide down their bed and trim Sickly Ploy's hair. Lose snippets of hair fell all around her bed, and once the five o'clock bell sounded, the first thing the ninth graders heard was an earth-shattering scream. Sickly Ploy was standing in front of the bathroom mirror, pale in the face, shivering. Her hair that was once kept in a cut resembling those of singers from the thoughtlessly named Kamikaze record label had been turned into an ear-length straight bob akin to those of lesser public schoolers.

'No. It can't be,' Sickly Ploy was still mumbling like someone who had completely lost her mind.

Those sleeping in the same zone began to gather around her. Then, as I was stretching my mattress cover, something fell down from underneath my pillow, hitting the floor with a *clank*.

## 3

'That bitch cut my hair! It's her!'

I stood still with the scissors in my hand.

Sickly Ploy believed that it was my doing. Everyone there believed that it was my doing. They held their hands up next to their mouths as they gossiped away like a group of noisy pigeons.

I was called to the office. Once I arrived, I saw that Sickly Ploy was already there, clutching her soaked handkerchief after crying so hard her eyes were puffy. That straight bob cut fit so perfectly with her silly look that I had to compliment her. 'That's pretty.'

She stared at me with fire in her eyes, reddened like a revengeful wraith. A middle-aged student affairs teacher cleared her throat and began the investigation.

'Did you cut your friend's hair?' she asked.

'I didn't,' I replied.

'Your friend said that you had threatened to cut her hair, and that everyone heard your threat.'

'I did say that, but I didn't do it.'

'A witness told me that you hid the scissors in your bed.'

'I have no idea how it was hidden there either.'

I only denied the crime, but didn't provide any excuses or useful information either. The teacher didn't believe me, but there was no solid evidence to hold me accountable. She tried approaching the matter from a different angle and asked what Sickly Ploy and I fought about prior to the event, to which Sickly Ploy didn't provide anything apart from her mumbles, '*she cut my hair, it's her*,' so neither did I.

Every ninth grader was waiting to see what kind of punishment I would receive—would my guardians be called in, or would I get suspended? When they saw me leaving the office just like that, they were bummed out. Sickly Ploy didn't waste any moment to stir up the matter.

'Oh please, how would she not be let off the hook? She was playing the victim, weeping like, "It wasn't me, please, teacher, it wasn't me." Well, that's all I can tell you. You have to see her face yourself, gosh, I almost threw up—that lying bitch.'

Those girls didn't hold Sickly Ploy in high regard to begin with—being friends with someone whose quality was just being a big mouth wouldn't improve your life in any way—but with hot drama served in front of you, who wouldn't join in the fun?

'Such a horrible person—not just a thief, but an envious one at that.'

'What a liar.'

'She's envious of your beautiful hair. That cockroach has such wiry hair it looks like a pot scrubber.'

The adjective to my name must have started taking shape from that remark; I turned into someone that the whole class abhorred. They planned to get back at me in secret, saying that they would slap me when they found the chance, put shampoo in my shoes, fill my locker with sand, and teach me my lesson. Still, no one dared to do any of that in broad daylight—no one had the guts to initiate it. In a manner similar to other girls' schools, they played a mind game with me with silence as their main weapon, leaving me to do work on my own when it was time for group projects. I remember all their faces, all those little devils who snickered when the teacher asked, 'which group has a spot left for one more friend,' or, 'there, that group isn't full yet—go join them, Ploy.' Those who I used to work with abandoned me, and it was around that time when I found a new work partner, Silent Ploy, whose story wasn't all that interesting so I'll save that for later.

And before you misunderstand me, I'm not telling you all this for your pity. I know how the minds of social animals that live in herds work—they need a mutual enemy to live in harmony, and I just happened to be at the perfect spot to play that role. That's it. I don't need any pity from anyone—I'm only telling you about this because the event that follows is just too darn juicy. The case of the hair trimmer isn't over yet, you see.

The second time it took place was during the night when I was away for a surgery to get gallstones removed.

## 4

The second victim, Ploy Sai, stood screaming in front of the mirror with her hands in her hair (which was an exact reproduction of Sickly Ploy's incident). Everyone looked at my bed. No one was there. The bed was neatly made without any traces of being used. The Cockroach wasn't there. Then, who was it? Who? Who?

'Did Cockroach's friend do it?'

The question only made the riddle harder to solve. No way, Cockroach had no friends, not a single one left, as they had made sure of that themselves. Who was it that committed the deed, then? Then began looking around for a mutual enemy again—someone who used to clash with Ploy Sai. Someone approached Ploy Sai and asked, 'Who do you think did it?'

'Paulie', Ploy Sai said softly. She wasn't a big mouth like Sickly Ploy, and Paulie was her best friend. 'Paulie once told me that she was envious of how the school allows me to wear my hair long as a special case because I have advertisements to film.'

'What did you say?!' Paulie waded her way through the crowd, seemingly ready for a fight. 'I did say that, but does that mean I'm the culprit? What nonsense.'

'Isn't it, though? You're always jealous of me because we are neighbours, and your family is poorer than mine. You have to use hand-me-downs from your older siblings, and you always get jealous when I have something new, not to mention how you think you're ugly . . . Ouch!' Before she could finish her sentence, her best friend had struck her across her face. She was stunned for a long moment, then she took a few steps back and threw herself at her friend, exchanging punches and slaps to the point that other dorm mates had to separate them.

'Let me go. Let me go—I'll slap that bitch!' Paulie roared.

'Let me go, I've always been annoyed by this cow. Let me give her a taste!' Ploy Sai shrugged away the classmates that tried to hold her back. In the end, both of them got sent to the office and were subsequently suspended.

I knew that there was a hushed whisper from among the crowd.

"What if Cockroach didn't cut Sickly Ploy's hair?"

Everyone had that thought, but a mutual enemy was still needed; as long as Cockroach remained the culprit in Sickly Ploy's incident, they could still trust one another. Even with Ploy Sai and Paulie's quarrel turning into a dark smudge within their hearts, they were all willing to believe that it had sprouted from a personal disagreement between the two.

### 5

Once I was permitted to leave the hospital, the school had already turned into a much scarier place. The change was obvious once I walked back into the classroom—some thirty pairs of eyes belonging to teenage girls pierced into me right at that instant.

They were much bolder with me, especially Sickly Ploy who had people at her back and dared to insult me with no fear of being snapped back at. I began receiving letters with malicious content in my locker, my personal belongings were stolen without a trace and replaced with rubbish or floor dust. It was impossible to look for clues of who did it—they were doing it in such complete concordance that it was impossible for our homeroom teacher or any student affairs teacher to intervene. Once asked about bullying, they would put on a surprised face and say, 'Our class really gets along great.' When someone asked about me, they would reply, 'Ploy is quiet and doesn't like to spend time with us, so we don't want to force her to.'

Even someone that seemed as innocent as Pretty Ploy—(Not Ploy Sai, did I make it confusing? I'm sorry that this story is filled with girls named Ploy, but it's not my fault for putting all of them together in one class.) Pretty Ploy never made it known whether she hated me or not, but she was close with her friends and too popular to take a stance against anything—she was too worried about her popularity going down, which was totally normal for a lower secondary schooler.

Well, during this one evening when the dinner bell sounded, I headed back to the class building to grab something. I saw a silhouette of a girl looking about my desk, picking pieces of paper out to throw into the bin. I swung the door open and startled the silhouette, which turned out to be everyone's sweetest Pretty Ploy.

Pretty Ploy laughed awkwardly and put her hands behind her back, feigning ignorance. I walked straight to the bin and picked up the paper she had thrown away to read.

'No, don't read them,' Pretty Ploy cried, but it was too late. That piece of paper was completely crumpled, a short message scribbled on it: I *hate you, you bitch. Why so shameless, Cockroach.*

I looked at Pretty Ploy and asked, 'Did you write this?'

Pretty Ploy shook her head rapidly. 'No, it wasn't me. I found it under your desk, so I was throwing it away for you.'

'What were you doing at my desk, then?'

I narrowed my eyes. She didn't tell me why and only kept on denying her involvement, which made me terribly annoyed.

'It just seems as if you felt bad that I saw you doing it, so you threw it away,' I said. 'If you wrote that, just admit it—everyone does that anyway. I'm just a bit disappointed to have believed that you're different from them. Or do you know who wrote it? You can just give me the name.'

Pretty Ploy gritted her teeth. I failed to make sense of the cause behind the tears welling up in her eyes—was it annoyance or fear to admit to the crime? She shouted back at me, 'Sure, I wrote it. You cockroach, I wrote it, do you hear me? Cockroach!'

I only watched on in pity as she stomped away. This pity would turn into empathy later on as I grew up and looked back at the past. What a pitiful girl, she had a pretty face so everyone must have fussed over her, and thus was never cornered like that.

Oh, well.

## 6

I still had to take school days off for check-ups at the hospital, during which the actual hair trimmer acted like an anti-hero, proving my innocence. Every morning after I was away from the dormitory, there would be a girl from class M 3/2 screaming in front of the dorm mirror, crying with her hair trimmed into a sorry state. The styles of the cut were different each time too.

What surprised me was, in complete harmony, each of them would have a certain culprit in their mind. And once they tried to narrow the list of suspects, the victim's finger would always be pointing at the best friend.

'Poito must be the one who did it, she's jealous that I got a letter from Phee Tarn, a senior she has a crush on. Why, Phee Tarn won't ever want you—her eyes are up here, not down here to look at someone so short.'

'Why did you cut my hair, Moody Ploy? Just because I became closer to Ploy Jah and not you?'

'What, you little bitch.'

'So, you're showing your true colours at last—a shoe would fit into your foul mouth perfectly.'

'No, don't fight, both of you.'

'Whoa, class M 3/2 is going at it again.'

'She's pinning the other girl down already.'

'Mrs Ploy, please hurry over here!'

'Stop right at this instant, girls!'

From harmonious classmates, they slowly turned into a lump of paranoia. Some of them refused to sleep just to preserve their hair, some pushed their beds together and took turns keeping watch until dawn. Still, it was to no avail—the hair trimmer would find a way to cut someone's hair. Some even borrowed an electric shaver to shave their hair short, allowing their hair to be at no one else's mercy.

Three months had passed with no progress made at the investigation into the case of hair trimmer, and the school began receiving complaints from the parents. However, there were less of those whose hair weren't yet trimmed as time went by. Then everything took a 180-degree turn: whoever hadn't got their hair trimmed yet would be lumped together as possible suspects. The victims of class M 3/2 were so invested in the case that they turned into detectives and had a few conspiracy theories under their belt.

During the middle of one night, I woke up to find Paula with beautiful brown hair sneaking away to turn on the light of the dorm's bathroom. The tell-tale *snip, snip* noise of hairdressing scissors could be heard. Then she cracked the door open, and a dimmed fluorescent light made uneven trims of hair on Paula's round head visible.

Once morning came, Paula stood crying in front of the mirror. 'With my hair so fucked up, I'd rather die.' She was going for the Academy Awards. I stood behind her, scowling and feeling somewhat triumphant for being the only one who could expose her. Your hair is wrapped up in a paper meant for sanitary pads and thrown away in the bin over there, you stupid one. And even if you flushed down your hair, there would still be traces of hair along the bathroom floor—I knew that you weren't that smart and simply wanted attention for yourself. Still, I held my tongue. I just wanted to know where this serial trimming of their own hair would end up.

The victims of the hair trimmer case must have known that Paula was putting on an act, but since they were in such a solidarity, they would accept anyone deemed a victim.

Just so they could remain 'the majority' of this small fishpond that was class M 3/2.

## 7

'Your head is still safe, isn't it?'

Silent Ploy looked up at me, the silence her answer: *Yes, it is. So, what of it?*

Silent Ploy was as quiet as her bestowed adjective, so quiet that she might as well be Muted Ploy. We only ever spent time together during group projects, outside of that, she would disappear from the classroom. She was friends with students from other classes whom I didn't know much about, only that they were otakus who spent time huddling around manga.

I rarely initiated conversations, but with Silent Ploy, she would always keep her silence if I didn't. When I asked her questions during our group projects, Silent Ploy would use her silence to show approval, and smile awkwardly if she was against my proposal. She would sometimes raise her brow, the corner of her mouth might twitch, and many other things that always required interpretation. Her presence was paper-thin; an invisible entity in the class, standing above all conflicts and never one to rejoice in love and harmony. Sometimes, I would think that she was cool for remaining so calm; and at other times, I would simply see her as one goofy girl.

'Your head is still safe, I see.' I only meant it as a joke. Of course, no one thought to cut Silent Ploy's hair because there was no point in doing so—Silent Ploy's hair had always been kept in a rulebook-abiding, bowl haircut ever since her first day of school. I rested my chin on my elbow, observing her, and proceeded to ask, amused, 'Say, you'll get in trouble if this continues, no? We are the last two people in this class with their same old hair.'

Silent Ploy was silent.

'You're already in enough trouble doing work with me, no?'

Silence.

'Do you want my help? To trim your hair like other people's?'

Silence.

'That was a joke. Try laughing for once, dumbass.'

'Let's,' Silent Ploy said at last, with a voice as hoarse as a boy's. My jaw dropped.

'Cut it for me,' she repeated her intention for the first time ever, looking at me with such a firm resolve that I couldn't say no to her.

That evening, I cut Silent Ploy's hair—I cut her a rule-breaking shaggy bob, the kind that she would never walk into a hair salon and ask for. It was not a covert act done in darkness; we did it for all to see, with every classmate's eyes upon us.

'There you go,' I puffed up the hair at the back of Silent Ploy's head. With that, the ever-dull Silent Ploy seemed more like a delinquent.

Silent Ploy looked at the mirror, turning her head left and right as she checked out her new haircut.

Silence.

Then a slow nod.

## 8

What followed was a rather strange turn of events that even I, looking back now as an outsider, fail to comprehend.

The bullying stopped right after that.

It stopped like, how should I put it . . . Just vanished, poof! Like the plague back in the Middle Ages that took one-third of the continent's population with it during its strides, then disappeared into thin air as if it never happened. I never got any apologies from anyone whatsoever, and no one ever asked me enthusiastically to join their group projects. I would sit still, like always, waiting for the teacher to announce, 'if any group's not full yet, please have your friend join you,' and only then would they look at each other in uneasiness and slowly raise a hand.

To be fair, they acted more reasonably towards me. Polite and at arm's length; a satisfactory silence that one shouldn't place their faith in. I was ever prepared should anything grim take place, but it never did.

Their ugly haircuts grew out near the end of the second semester, and once the finals came, the ninth graders got their last haircuts before they would be allowed to wear their hair long in their upper secondary years. Some grew fond of the short shags that the culprit left them and never wore their hair long again, while some realized that their lives were much easier with rule-abiding bobs and chose to continue wearing one. The stories were fading away. No one dug it up to discuss any more. The perpetrator was never caught. And Sickly Ploy continued to believe that I was the one who cut her hair.

Then it was time for our graduation from ninth grade. Our homeroom teacher had us take a class photo together, which I received via post during the summer break and threw into the bin right away. My mom thought that I had thrown it away by accident and retrieved it for me, so I had to shred it into pieces and set it on fire so as to not ever see that photo again.

I took an admission exam into another high school, one whose academic ranking was behind my former school, but I was old enough to rent a fifteen-square-metre room in Bangkok to live on my own.

'Why won't you continue studying at the same school, honey? I have enough money for the tuition fees, you know,' my mom said. 'Were the classes too hard? Did you have any problems with your friends?'

'That doesn't have anything to do with it,' I replied.

Mom smiled and stroked my wiry hair. 'Do you know, Ploy? When I was looking for a school for you, I ended up choosing a boarding school because you were such a quiet child during elementary school. I wanted you to have friends, and the teacher who gave me a school tour told me that it was the correct decision—the school's selling point was how they taught their students to love each other, and that their students were always living in perfect harmony.'

I snorted. How should I answer this?

'That they did. I just wasn't cut out for it.'

## 9

It had been one year since I started my life anew in a place where no one knew me. No one called me cockroach here, but they opted for Noodle Ploy instead (because my hair was curly like instant noodles, the one who gave me the name explained). I didn't like the name, but I could only laugh—no name could possibly be worse than Cockroach, could it?

What I came to learn was, there always would be problems wherever you were. I always found myself in arguments with my friends to the point of going separate ways almost on a daily basis; still, these 'problems' always had their own conclusions. These conflicts simply needed to be solved through talking and agreeing on terms acceptable to both parties, unlike that dragged-on psychological warfare. The feeling as if you have to struggle to stay afloat was no more, either.

I went to tutoring classes to prepare for university entrance exams, and the striking colour of my old school's uniform skirt always had me turning my head around. The upper secondary schoolers from our boarding school could ask for a special permission to leave the dorm to attend tutoring schools, so I got to meet some old friends at these buildings. They continued to live in herds, each of them grown up so much that I hardly recognized them. Their child-like cheek fat was gone. Someone's big velvety hair ribbon whipped so close to my face that I had to take a step to the side.

The one who almost bumped into me bowed their head a bit to apologize, and it was only after I heard her voice that I remembered her as Pretty Ploy—the one who snuck pieces of paper from underneath my desk into the bin, the one who confessed to having written insults directed at me.

'Actually, I know who wrote it—it was my best friend. I saw her writing you bad words, telling you to go die. I couldn't take it but didn't have the courage to stop her, so I grabbed it from your desk. When you blamed me for it even though I was actually trying to help you, I was angry,' she confessed to me during the break before the next class in the tutoring school.

We sat and talked in a smoothie shop with just the two of us. Pretty Ploy offered to pay for my drink, to which I refused, which in turn made her feel somewhat hurt. However, we continued with our chat. She began with simple questions: how was the new school, and whether they were any cute boys. I asked about old friends and found out that nearly half of the students from our year left to continue their upper secondary education elsewhere, and those who were once in class M 3/2 went to different classrooms for different academic programmes, so what was once a secret was no more.

During our talk, I noticed that Pretty Ploy was avoiding any mentions of a certain event time after time. I rested my chin on my elbow, letting her take her time, and it was her who let it slip at last.

'I was the one who cut Sickly Ploy's hair,' Pretty Ploy said. 'She got on my nerves—do you know that everyone hated Sickly Ploy? She had a big mouth, always picking fights, and always had this excuse that she was sick whenever someone said mean stuff to her. No one wanted to be her friend any more in high school.'

'Why cut her hair, then? There were so many things to choose from.'

'Well, you threatened her in the craft workshop, so I found it convenient,' she muttered, only to quickly correct herself once she probably realized that it was self-incriminating. 'Everyone did—it was the chance to do it.'

I couldn't contain my laughter. 'There's no need to feel sorry for me, then!'

'No, listen.' Pretty Ploy became increasingly agitated just like the last time. 'I just wanted to teach Sickly Ploy a lesson, so she would keep her mouth shut and leave you alone in the process. However, the whole thing turned out the other way around. But, but . . . it wasn't my fault. I should've stopped them from being mean to you, but I didn't want to get roped into it, so I . . .'

'How about we stop there, miss pageant queen with a skeleton in her cupboard; the more you talk, the more

I feel pity for you. Just think about what you've just said when you get home and see for yourself how bad it sounded—you're now more pitiful than Sickly Ploy.'

With that, I grabbed my bag and got up to leave. Pretty Ploy was so furious her whole body was shaking. She yelled after me, 'You aren't a saint either, you damn cockroach! You really stole someone else's stuff; I saw it with my own two eyes.'

I let out a long sigh and said, 'Whether I was a thief or not doesn't validate your act.'

'Gosh, stop playing victim, what I'm saying is—' Pretty Ploy looked up, looked down, and then up again. She struggled to cough up each word from her pretty throat. 'I even admitted my wrongdoings with you because I want to be your friend, to correct our misunderstandings and reconcile with you, then why . . . why?'

'But I'm not your friend,' I cut our conversation short. 'I don't want to be friends with a madwoman so drunk on power to the point of assuming the role of a vigilante and cutting your classmates' hair in the dark.'

'That wasn't me!'

'Who was it, then?'

Pretty Ploy couldn't provide me with an answer. Hence, the case of hair trimmer became one of those unsolved cases within the grounds of that girls' school. It was abandoned alongside the case of the mysterious phone call that ordered twenty pizzas to be delivered to the office of student affairs, and the case where one whole pond of koi was poisoned, all of which would turn into a funny story when you recount the events to your friends later on in life. However, back then, they never were funny; they were gravely serious, just like how the school once was a teenager's whole world.

'The students in your school seem to hate each other a lot.'

My high school friend told me thus once I finished recounting the case of the hair trimmer. Her simple words surprised me—I knew that everyone there hated me, but I never imagined that they would hate each other as well. They hated each other but couldn't possibly live without each other nor make it known that they hated one another, for they were dictated to be in perfect harmony. If they were to hate each other openly, it would be much easier than donning masks and socializing. If they were to openly fight with each other, they might not have to suffer fake friendships like the one that Pretty Ploy tried to offer me.

Now that I think about it, we really complicated things too much back then.

# Hirun and Beardy

**'Do you know that I used to like you so damn much?'**

Regardless of the turn of events that led up to this point, if you were to ask Hirun, he would probably tell you that he was simply drunk and talking nonsense. If you were to ask Beardy, he would tell you that drunk people never lie, and that hundreds of secrets locked within one's heart could be freed with a sip of alcohol. On the other hand, if you readers were to ask me, I would say: whatever, it's too late to be saying that now anyway.

## 1: Hirun

It all started with a whiff of cigarette smell.

Lately, Hirun began to notice that Saeng, his nephew who was currently in eleventh grade, had begun to smoke behind his back, and it was the cigarettes that Hirun had carefully hidden beneath a DVD player to boot. 'Cigarettes are bad,' he was about to lecture, but once his nephew revealed that the cigarettes were his own, Hirun couldn't bring himself to. Not to swipe his cigarettes to smoke? To know the difference between children and grown-ups? His

nephew would say that he was stinky! So, Hirun decided
to hand his cigarettes out to the employees of his bar
and the postman. 'Let's call it even,' he told his nephew.
'I'll stop smoking, and you don't go searching for them
yourself, okay?'

His nephew tilted his head, pretending to heed to
his words, but he knew right away from the gesture that
the boy was planning to defy him. This was Saeng that
he was talking to, the child who ran away from home on
the enrolment day of the upper secondary school that
was the hardest to get into in the whole country, and all
that was done just to spite his family. It was a safe bet
that his nephew would come back home with the smell
of cigarettes clinging to his clothes sometime this week.

Why, Hirun didn't need to wait a week. Just two days
later his nephew was marching around in his bar with a
cigarette hanging from his lips.

'That table gave it to me.' His nephew blew the smoke
in a beautiful doughnut shape without a care in the world.

'Didn't I tell you not to go around begging for
cigarettes from grown-ups?' Hirun screeched.

'I didn't beg. I won them fair and square.'

'What are you talking about?'

'Pocketing all eight balls.'

'Who said you could have a pool match with the
patrons?!'

Saeng pretended like he didn't hear him. And before
anyone asks who taught the boy to play pool, it was
him, wasn't it?! Hirun ran out of words and could only
slump down next to his nephew, asking a question that

any and all parents would frown upon hearing. 'Do you have another one?' Thus, an old uncle and his nephew who was not of legal age blew cigarette smoke together underneath the bar's dim yellow lights. It was quite a sight, one that cops should have been called upon.

Yes, the whole thing started off with the smell of a cigarette, the same cigarette that he had asked his nephew for. It had the same scent as Hirun's first cigarette ever—cherry, perhaps? Hirun thought. Yes, cherry. He couldn't be wrong. What a snob. The one who handed him the cigarette, the towering giant with a bushy beard like Che Guevara's, black leather jacket, a big bike, and words from wuxia dramas that poured forth from his mouth whenever he talked.

What did the guy say? The words that made him cringe to his backbone?

Oh.

*One day, Hirun, you'll be dying to smell this again.*

'Dying.'

'What did you say?' Saeng raised his brows.

'Who? Who said what? I didn't.' Hirun was so darn agitated.

'Who was dying?'

'Saeng.' Hirun cleared his throat, crossed his arms and put on a serious face, self-assured that his cool look was absolutely convincing. Cherry cigarettes, is it? He knew that it couldn't possibly be, but it would be better to ask than to let it go. He asked his nephew what the one who gave him the cigarettes looked like.

'Nothing remarkable, really,' Hai Saeng said the first sentence just to mess with his uncle. The real answer, however, followed: 'Plain, seemed gullible, like an office worker that would lose all their money to a phone scam.'

'Did he have a beard? Ear piercings? How long was his hair?'

'No beard, very simple short hair, and a dumb face like your usual office workers. He had a bit of a beer belly and wore this striped shirt.'

His nephew even stressed on the word 'dumb'. Hirun laughed. All right, it couldn't be him. It couldn't possibly be.


## 2: Beardy

As I, your writer, don't know nor care enough about the name of that man from Hirun's memory, I will refer to him as Beardy.

True to the description that the seventeen-year-old boy had relayed to his uncle, Beardy had no beard—used to, but had been long without one ever since he shaved it all off for his university graduation. At first, Beardy wasn't used to his clean-shaven face that no longer exuded an air of dominance, but it was due to this missing feature that the company whose open position he had applied for didn't throw his résumé into a dustbin—it was due to this well-scrubbed handsomeness that a senior from the accounting department came to flirt with him at his desk every day.

We won't go too deep into Beardy's life as an office worker, as it's too darn boring in my opinion. Let's just say that Hirun used to call him Beardy because the man once had a beard, and that they used to ride their big bikes along rural roads that hugged the woods and the hills when they were young, and sleep wherever the sun set upon them. Those sweet memories (which aren't quite literally sweet—more like dank from sweat) from their university days faded with time. The job hunt consumed Beardy's life, and Hirun stopped contacting him; neither of them knew how the other had been doing.

Beardy's client told him to meet up at a jazz house with a weird name, located in the outskirts of the city. 'The Tempest', Beardy read its name. *How cool.* So *damn rock*, and not befitting the entrance to the place that was more like a small house bursting with green foliage, where passers-by could hear piano tunes drifting in the air at night. Hirun had once said that he wanted his own store, the thought crossed Beardy's mind, and he reckoned that if the man ever did, it would perhaps look like this.

'Eh? You can't make it any more? Of course, that's all right. Well . . . I'm at the place already, but I can head back—it's no problem. I'll see you later.'

And what a coincidence it was that his client had to cancel the meeting when the female waitress brought him a plate of fish sauce chicken wings. *Great.* He couldn't leave now and had to order a drink to accompany the plate of food instead. Beardy asked for some Jack Daniels, and the waitress shouted the order at someone behind the counter bar. 'Nong Saeng, dear, could you bring a glass of Jack on the rocks for our customer?' She smiled at him, then a short while after, *Nong Saeng* approached him and placed a tray in front of Beardy.

*A kid?*

It was weird enough for a child under eighteen to work in a bar, but there was something weirder still. Beardy furrowed his brows. Be it his face, his eyes, the way he picked stuff up—the boy was exuding such a familiar presence that Beardy saw images from bygone days fitting perfectly onto him.

*This boy—is this a downsized Hirun?*

'What are you looking at, huh?' Once he realized that he was being stared at, the boy narrowed his eyes in a hostile manner.

And there, Beardy was snapped right back from his trance with those words. Hirun, according to the memory from his freshman year in university, looked just like this, but the man had a much nicer temperament . . . Regardless, this similarity couldn't possibly be a coincidence, and thus Beardy decided to ask the boy, 'Who are your parents?'

'Huh?'

'Excuse me for asking this, but what's your dad's name?'

'You want to know my father?' The boy grinned, his tone of voice when he uttered '*my father*' was dripping with unmasked hatred. Still, the boy allowed him to be privy to his father's first name and surname. The name sounded familiar to him—perhaps some famous attorney, but whatever.

'And what's your name?' he asked as he shook his packet of cherry cigarettes for one of them to fall out. 'I heard her calling you Nong Saeng, can I call you that?'

'Why are you so persistent to know more about me? Yuck.' Nong Saeng pointed at the pool table. 'Play Eight Ball with me. I'll tell you if you win.'

'Wait—'

'If I do, I want that.' The boy pointed at the cigarette in his hand.

'Um . . .'

Without a single chance to catch his breath, Beardy was obliterated. The whole pack of cigarettes became the property of the local boy. Still, said boy wasn't as cruel as he seemed to be, for he allowed the man to know his name, at least.

'Hirun,' the boy said with a smile and walked away with a cigarette between his lips, leaving Beardy alone at the pool table, stunned.

The chicken wings were cold, and the ice cubes in that glass of Jack Daniels had already melted. Beardy asked the waitress for the bill and hurried home.

*What the hell.*

Just one word—just one single name and it kept Beardy awake the whole night: Hirun. A two-syllable name and a face that was identical to another's. Beardy tossed and turned in his bed, grabbed his mobile phone to search for Hirun's name on Facebook, and could only sigh. The result remained the same as years ago: he was blocked.

No explanations. No cause. Out of nowhere, Hirun blocked him from his life—Facebook, phone number, none of them reachable. He tried contacting him through his friends, only to find out that Hirun had no other friends he was close with. Beardy couldn't make any sense of all this—*what in the hell is this one-sided separation?*

Beardy visited 'The Tempest' time after time after that night, looking around for Hirun—no, not Hirun in the guise of that weird child whose intention was to rile him up . . . He was looking for the real Hirun, the friend his age, perhaps thirty-four or thirty-five years old by then. He was utterly convinced that if mini-Hirun was there, then Hirun must be nearby.

However, Beardy wasn't aware of one fact: the Hirun that he was looking for was the owner of the place. The owner would not be walking around, serving deep-fried chicken wings and filling up their ice stock. The owner would be sitting in the second-floor office, focused on accounting tasks and only reared his head out nearing the closing time or whenever he was in the mood to play some piano—the latter of which was really rare. And as my dear readers must have learned from the previous section, Hirun didn't know that the dumb-looking office worker was Beardy, so he had no mind to make his face known at all.

### 3: Hirun

With neither of them noticing the presence of the other after so long, your author deemed that the story ought to progress at a quicker pace. Hence, the following events happened abruptly.

'Uncle, a customer invited me on a trip.'

Hirun fell from his chair right at the moment his nephew came to make the announcement. *Why so abruptly?*

'No way!'

'I'm not asking for permission—I'm just letting you know.'

'Where to?!'

Saeng chuckled and said that his uncle was weird to deny him outright even before he had told him the destination.

'Doi Samer Dao,' his nephew replied. Hirun had heard its name before. Doi Samer Dao was in Nan province, one of the many destinations Beardy and he had planned to visit on their big bikes after graduation. However, things always came up and they had to take a rain check time after time; they ended up never getting to make the trip until the day Hirun decided to block Beardy.

Hirun held his breath as he asked, 'What's the name of this customer?'

'No idea,' Hai Saeng replied, deadpan.

'Didn't you say that this person's a regular? How come you don't know?'

'Well, they aren't interesting enough for me to ask.'

'And you said yes just so?'

'Yup.'

'Saeng, you . . .' Hirun massaged the area between his brows with mixed feelings. 'I know that you aren't naive enough for an adult to lure you away, so why don't you tell me what you're planning.'

As per usual, Hirun tried to outwit his nephew. He thought that he had caught up to his nephew already, but Saeng remained ever the same—the boy simply shrugged and told his uncle to drop him off at the bus terminal station next week at five in the evening.

Hirun was extremely annoyed. 'What? They asked you to join them on a trip, and you guys are taking a tour bus?

What about the accommodation? Haven't booked any yet? How dare you not make any itinerary—have I ever brought you through such hardship? Have you thought of what to do after you step off the bus? This person's already a grown-up, so why don't they drive you there and put up a camping tent? You go tell that customer that everything's off the table—I can bring my nephew on trips myself. Go, go tell that person right away.'

Saeng raised his brow, but he still complied and headed downstairs from his uncle's office. Hirun sighed, then a thought crossed his mind: *Why don't I go sort out the matter myself?* Letting Saeng off alone like this, the boy might pull some weird stunt again—no one knew what kind of evil plan might be brewing in his beloved nephew's head. And who was this customer? They were in no way close, yet this person had decided to bring his nephew on a trip—he must go see their face.

But once he caught up to Saeng at the bar, he only found the boy smoking a cigarette alone next to the pool table.

'Where's that customer?' Hirun asked.

'Headed back just now, but we did sort the matter out.'

*Sort the matter out?* 'What did you tell him?'

'That we do everything as planned, plus, you'll be driving for us.'

'Huh?!'

Hirun nearly bit his tongue. *This boy—what an unreliable messenger.*

'And he said,' Saeng was almost unable to contain his laughter at this point, 'that dumb office worker—he said: I'll see you, Hirun.'

*I'll see you, Hirun.*

*I'll see you.*

*Hirun.*


**'We take a right at the next junction.'**

'Oh, wait, right is for the main street—we're staying away from the city. Take the left.'

'It's not the holiday season—why take the roundabout route? That road's narrow.'

'Come on, it's wide enough.'

'That road only has two lanes—"wide enough" only applies to motorcycles. Have you ever driven a car before, old man?'

'Ah, that's true. I'm sorry, Hirun. Right it is then.'

His nephew sighed, muttering that he never thought their companion would be such a baggage.

*What the heck.*

*What?*

*What's this?*

He didn't understand a single thing, if anyone would be so kind as to enlighten him?

First, why was Beardy in his car?

Second, why was Beardy friends with Saeng?

Third . . .

'Hirun.'

'Huh?' / 'Uh-huh?'

Why would his sorry excuse of a nephew answer Beardy whenever he called his name?

The bigger Hirun glanced at the smaller Hirun. His dear nephew sat there without a care in the world, and not looking regretful in the slightest at not giving his uncle an explanation that was long overdue. On the day the boy would go on the trip, Beardy would show up out of nowhere with a sleeping bag and a camping tent, then proceed to hop into the backseat of his car. Saeng was sitting in the passenger seat next to Hirun, looking at the GPS map on his phone while choosing the next song. Whatever the boy's mood might be, he chose a song from the coming-of-age romantic movie, *My Girl*.

*With hearts aligned, new love is found. How happy am I to fall in love.*

*The heart's with you; the mind's on cloud nine.*

*Should you wait there, I'd be pleased.*

*Pleased? Like hell I am!* Hirun snapped back in his mind as his eyes went to the rearview mirror. This plain-looking office worker in casual clothes suited for hiking was without a doubt Beardy; the man had changed quite a lot now that he no longer wore Ray-Ban glasses, and the reserved, cool air that came with a studded leather jacket was gone; what was left was a thirty-four-year-old man with a large frame who lacked confidence, yet was packed full with a slightly crooked back from office syndrome and a beer belly. However, even with the absence of his beard, that smug side profile and the pair of melancholic eyes like Wong Kar-wai's male lead were enough to remind Hirun at first glance.

A mess of emotions took hold of Hirun's heart during the eight hours he painstakingly drove the car for. He had no courage to talk to his old friend; cumbersome memories of the past made themselves known one after the other, bringing to mind that one last word from

Beardy that had made Hirun sever the relationship he had with the man. Beardy, too, seemed to be aware of the fact that he wasn't welcome. He talked to Hirun through Saeng, telling the boy to tell his uncle to make a pit stop whenever he needed to use the toilet, and simply nudged him again when it was time for food. They stopped for some rice soup along the way, a bowl each, and two for Beardy. They had no trouble ordering food to share, but Hirun was still lacking the courage to meet Beardy's eyes. *We aren't close any more—I'm just here to keep my nephew company*, Hirun thought as he stole a glance at his old friend's sleeping face. He was planning to make himself as invisible as possible, so that he wouldn't have to talk to Beardy throughout the trip.

As you must be aware, there would be some kind of deus ex machina that your author deemed necessary for the man's plot to fail miserably; for example, how Saeng stopped his role as the navigator when Hirun took a turn uphill near sunset. Hirun looked over at the boy, his brows furrowed.

'The internet's out,' Saeng said, 'but the camping ground shouldn't be far-off, no? You should be able to manage that.'

'Of course . . . not,' Hirun whined. He had never been up this mountain, and during his days as a biker, he only needed to turn around if he took the wrong road. Now that he was responsible for the lives of his two companions, the pressure was crushing him.

Along with the weight of his old friend's palm that landed on Hirun's shoulder.

'Park somewhere.' Beardy, who had just woken up, drowsily shoved his face between their seats. 'Young Hirun, change seats with me. I'll take your seat.'

'You know the way?' Saeng narrowed his eyes sceptically.

'It's my domain from here on.' Beardy stroked his beard, pleased by his own radiance.

Saeng covered his mouth, nauseated by the words. If it was years back, Hirun would have been searching for a puke bucket too; but this time around, his heart was pounding.

## 4: Beardy

It all began days ago, while Beardy was sipping his third glass of whiskey and listening to the piano song by the boy that was parading around like he was the place's manager. 'It's "Kiss the Rain",' the waitress whispered the name to him; he didn't know the song, but it was so damn beautiful that his heart was swayed along with its melancholic tunes. Beardy had to admit that the boy was great—his fingers did wonders at delivering the sweetest song in contrast to each painful remark that left the boy's mouth.

'Hey, old man, do you like my uncle?'

There, the boy stabbed him to the hilt the moment he reached his table.

Beardy feigned ignorance and asked who the boy's uncle was, at which the boy laughed and brought his phone up to show him a video clip. It was a video from some random night where Beardy was in a drunken stupor, and it was such a bad one that he had held on to the boy's sleeve, preventing him from walking away. His lips were muttering incoherently, yet few words could be made out: 'Hirun, no, fuck, don't leave me.'

The boy put his phone away in his pocket and crossed his arms as he waited for an answer. Heat rushed to Beardy's face, reaching his ears. Having succumbed to the evidence provided, he half-heartedly answered, 'Your uncle and I used to be very close.'

'Why "used to"?' the boy prodded again.

'No idea,' Beardy said. This past image of Hirun, his once closest friend, was always clear in his mind's eye; one with a handsome face and a strong will, yet most kind. Beardy was once kicked out by a hostel owner in the middle of the night because he was snoring so loud that other people who shared the same dorm room couldn't sleep, but Hirun who slept next to him never stirred from his slumber thanks to his earplugs; the man always had earplugs with him ever since he had learned that his friend snored in his sleep, and it was this tolerating way of cohabiting with his companion that left such a huge impression on Beardy.

'Then, why aren't you two together now?'

Why, indeed.

They finally reached the camping ground after wasting much time circling around the entrance, thanks to Beardy who had reserved a spot at a private camping ground, which wasn't what its advertisement had promised, being nearly half a kilometre away from the stargazing spot.

'A regular my ass—are we stargazing or going on an adventure? Who in their right mind would go half a kilometre uphill to stargaze in the middle of the night, then trek back down through the forest? Think, just think about it!'

'Sorry, I usually came here alone so I went for the cheapest one.'

'Unbelievable, old man . . .'

'I'm sorry. So sorry.'

After thirty minutes of being chided by both Uncle Hirun and Nephew Hirun, Beardy decided to give up his deposit money and showed them the way to another private plantation on the same mountain. This time around, everything went smoothly—Hirun was happy, and the nephew was happy—for which Beardy was somewhat glad, but he couldn't help thinking that the man had never grumbled no matter how far he had him trek; Hirun was either used to a comfortable life now, or the man was simply getting old. Beardy tried to brush his musings away—the view of mountain ranges at sunset was too beautiful for him to muddle his heart with nonsense. Hirun and Beardy put up the camping tents together while Hirun's nephew told them that he would go rent a sitting mat and a grill. Once the boy was gone, Hirun finally looked at him as he talked to him for the first time in many years. 'When you said that you're a regular here, did you mean that you've been here before?'

Beardy was stunned for a moment, each word leaving his lips with the greatest effort. 'Actually, I have been here many times.'

'I see. With your wife?' Hirun looked at him and smiled, but it was obvious to Beardy.

It was obvious that his once dear friend was annoyed by the answer.

At the plantation's camping ground, there were a lot of people setting up their camping tents. Hirun's Mongolian barbeque with two packs of minced pork flavoured noodles left them so full they could hardly move. The sun had long set behind the horizon, and the moonless night allowed for stars to light up the sky, twinkling. It was so damn romantic, so romantic that Beardy wanted to deliver his trademarke cheesy soliloquy: A *blanket of stars leaves one's heart yearning; clad in your burning love would perhaps keep me warm.* Beardy could imagine the looks on his two companions' faces if he were to say it out loud. Truth be told, he was fully aware of how he used to say cheesy lines on a daily basis; he simply enjoyed the reactions from others. He enjoyed how they pleaded him to stop: *That's fucking cheesy, please stop—stop with your 'the one who keeps my love true is the one my heart calls out to', your 'a heart's fever makes one's love sweeter', and your 'where there's a will, there's a woe'—just stop!*

Hirun's nephew stretched his hand out, asking for a cigarette from him. He gave the boy one and was surprised that Hirun didn't only let the boy take the cigarette in silence, but the man also stretched out his hand for one himself. After Hirun's nephew had finished the cigarette, the boy went to sleep. The night belonged to the adults after eleven o'clock; Hirun opened a can of beer and handed it to Beardy—what could beat a can of cold beer, fresh from an ice bucket at the top of a freezing mountain?

Beardy stole a glance at his old friend. Hirun returned the gaze.

'Why did you block me back then?' Beardy asked.

Hirun forced a smile; ever since the man had hopped into his car, he had prepared himself to face this question. Still, with Hirun being Hirun, he shared the same stubbornness born from the very same genetics as Saeng, his dear nephew. He kept his silence and downed the beer in place of an answer.

'Hirun,' Beardy prodded.

Hirun laughed dryly. 'Do you really not remember why?'

'I have no idea, really,' Beardy admitted. 'We last saw each other just a bit after I landed a job, right? We hung out like usual back then.'

'Yes, like usual, and what came next?'

'You told me that your family needed you for some family business, and that it'll be harder to meet up. Was that the cause?'

'No. Not even close.'

'How about you stop drinking for now? That's your third can already.'

'Mind your own business. Are we gonna talk or not?'

'Yes.'

Just to face this topic that he had turned his back on for a decade, Hirun needed a copious amount of alcohol. The clueless Beardy could only wonder: *Was I too smelly? Did I snore so loud that you couldn't stand it? Did I say too many cheesy lines? Or was I no longer cool without my beard?* The fourth can of beer was finished. Hirun squashed it in his palm and asked, 'What did you ask of me when we last met?'

Beardy furrowed his brows as he dug deep into his memory, then he let out an 'oh'.

'I asked you to be my best man at my wedding.'

Hirun smirked. 'That's it.'

'What's wrong with being my best man? Of course, I would want the most important person in my life as my best man—that's the most important role during my most important moment,' Beardy kept prodding. 'Why? Did you not like Nittaya? Or was there someone you didn't wanna meet? Why didn't you just tell me that you couldn't go?'

'Ugh. Are you stupid or stupid?'

'Really, I'm honestly asking you. I didn't think that it would be that much of a problem—you kept me blocked for ten years.'

'Gosh, Beardy. What a moron you are.'

'Hirun.'

'I'm out. I'm off to bed. See you tomorrow.'

'Hirun.'

'I liked you! Are you happy now?! I could put up with your shitty personality, and you went off to get married to an accountant girl! Then you had the audacity to invite me to be your best man—you must be so damn happy, right? And what's with Doi Samer Dao? You must have been here on your own time after time, no? This place that you had promised to come with me—this place that I left untouched just to visit with you. Damn you.'

Hirun let it all out now that he was drunk. He meant to bombard Beardy with a huge piece of his mind and escape into the tent that he had set up for his nephew and himself, but once he laid his eyes on said tent, he was frozen in place.

Saeng had already claimed the tent for his own, and his alone; the tent's entrance was zipped up from the inside.

## 5: Hirun

*It's all over—this hit-and-run plan.*

It took five minutes for Beardy to put away the empty cans, after which he followed Hirun and found the man shell-shocked in front of the tent. His face had reddened from the alcohol and his own embarrassment, even while his body shook, fighting against the mountain breeze that was some ten degrees Celsius. Seeing that, Beardy could only feel sorry for his friend and refrained from making any jokes to save whatever pride the man had left, so he only proceeded to pat Hirun's shoulder and pointed to his own camping tent. With no choice left, Hirun complied and followed him into the tent.

They laid down with their backs to each other underneath the same sleeping bag that was spread out to function as a blanket, both keeping their silence just like an old married couple that had fought over a trivial matter. Still, sleep visited neither of them; Hirun's small movements troubled Beardy's mind, while Beardy's attempt to scratch his own feet alone yanked at Hirun's heartstrings. *Stop moving, damn it,* was the thought that crossed both their minds over and over, completely unaware that the shuffling noise wasn't what was troubling them, but rather the confession that was drifting still in their hearts.

This time around, Beardy was the first to speak. 'Hirun.'

'Hmm?'

'You really used to like me?'

'Uh-huh. I did,' Hirun said, softly, 'back then.'

'Not any more?'

'Not any more. You can rest assured.'

This 'not any more' was so bitter in Hirun's throat, but he had to say it out loud, lest he forever feel guilty towards Beardy's wife. Of course, he knew full well that Beardy never once thought of him as more than a friend that came equipped with 100 per cent manly friendship, but he couldn't find it in his heart to dump his own baggage on to the man and run away yet again. Hirun swallowed the bitter lump forming in his throat. So, *this is the taste of lies mixed with tears.*

Regardless of the turn of events that led up to this point, if we were to ask Hirun once again tomorrow, he would probably tell us that he was simply drunk and talking nonsense, then smile a loser's smile as always. *You don't have to worry about that,* he would tell his friend. However, if we were to ask Beardy, he would tell us that drunk people never lie, and that hundreds of secrets locked within one's heart could be freed with a sip of alcohol.

Hirun heard a sob, and he hurriedly held his breath, having thought that the sound was his. Then, he realized, *no,* tears were streaming down Hirun's face, but he wasn't sobbing like that—the one sobbing was Beardy.

'And what in the hell are you crying for?!' Hirun, who wanted to scream at the top of his lungs but was still mindful of those sleeping in the neighbouring tents, pushed the blanket away as his patience snapped in half.

He saw Beardy curling up, his face buried in his hands, shaking like an abandoned baby.

'Well, you . . . You don't like me any more,' Beardy mumbled almost inaudibly. 'You left me alone for ten years just to tell me that you don't like me any more.'

'Huh?' Hirun felt as if all vocabulary had left his brain, and he was only capable of thinking, '*What? What the hell . . .*'

'What do you want from me, Beardy? I'm supposed to be the one crying, not you who was stupid enough to not realize another's feelings and asked him to be your best man, and then you had the audacity to return as a married man.'

Beardy looked up. 'Yeah, I had a wife, and divorced her too.'

'Stop talking nonsense.'

'You only knew me until the day I was about to get married, that's why. But that doesn't matter—I think my marriage started to fall apart as far back as the wedding day.'

Beardy hugged his pillow like a high school girl, which totally warranted a good kick in Hirun's eyes.

Once Hirun chose to disappear from his life, it was only then that Beardy had come to realize how important of a piece Hirun was in his life. That was the truth.

*What should I do? If I chase after him and find him, how should I ask him to return?*

However, Beardy's feelings from back then weren't as solid as Hirun's that he might loudly proclaim that he liked another man in a romantic way. Beardy's feelings were just a foggy, colourful lump of something that was akin to some dusty abstract art in a gallery; it was just like gunpowder that wasn't yet sent into the sky to burst into a firework. He went out with Nittaya, a girl from the accounting department, and he was serious about the relationship to the point of getting married to her. He could say it with ease back then that he loved her, but with Hirun, who never made any intentions to develop their relationship into something else known, his feelings were too muddled to be translated into words, hence the obscured state of things as they were.

Moreover, Hirun had never told him why he had disappeared.

Did Hirun hate him already?

No way.

Would Hirun stop being mad at him and eventually come back?

Once the wedding day arrived, Beardy hesitated.

Once it was time to perform the duty of a married couple, his member remained limp.

Once he began his married life with his wife, Beardy was always awkward and hesitant about every single thing. Nittaya commented that her husband had changed—*boring, unreliable, hesitant*—and Beardy accepted all her criticisms. He could no longer imagine his once cool and confident self, the long-haired man with a thick beard who always wore a leather jacket and a green Aviator Ray-Ban, the man who was always bathed in the alluring scent of cherry cigarettes. Hirun hadn't left with bare hands; Hirun had torn half of his being away with him, leaving Beardy behind with this overwhelming sense of *wrongness*. Beardy didn't allow himself to be happy, so the one sharing his life never tasted happiness just the same.

'Nittaya left me just two years in,' Beardy summarized. 'And I have been coming here every year because I missed you, and I was hoping I would bump into you—something like that.'

'Like hell you would—did you think that I left you to build a resort on a mountain? I did tell you to stop watching soap operas, didn't I?' Hirun kicked his friend, and Beardy whimpered. The man had already cried his eyes dry and was obviously tired.

Hirun scratched his head, feeling ashamed of his own wrinkle-riddled face and Beardy's alike. They were no longer teenagers, and here they were, doing things in a roundabout way, fighting over nothing; his nephew would surely give him a piece of his mind if they kept this up.

'Are you tired?' Hirun asked, and Beardy nodded in response. 'If so, then go to sleep already.'

'Hirun.'

'Hmm?'

Beardy poked at his hand with his finger and said in a hushed voice, 'I like you, always did, and still like you even now.'

' . . . '

'It's okay if you don't like me any more, but if that's all right with you, then we . . .'

' . . . '

'Hirun?'

Hirun was frozen in place.

'Uh . . . Are you okay? Uncomfortable? I can sleep outside, you know.'

Hirun remained silent. Beardy shot up.

'I'm leaving.'

'Stay here.'

'. . .'

'Stay here, go to sleep already.'

'Hirun.'

'Be quiet.'

'Hirun.'

'I told you to shut your mouth, are you really that dumb?'

'Uh . . . Do you have your earplugs?'

'I didn't bring them.'

'Then please endure for a night, that's all I wanna say.'

At that, Beardy flopped back down and went to sleep. He was snoring so loudly that the whole campground might have woken because of the noise alone, ready to give him a piece of their mind.

*Nice.* Hirun was relieved that Beardy's snores were loud enough to drown out the sound of his hammering heart.

*But that's too damn loud!*

'Beardy. Damn Beardy, wake up. I can't sleep.'

*Zzz . . .*

Hirun got up and grabbed on to his old pal's shoulder, then slapped it for the man to turn to the side. *Come on, sleep on your side now.*

*This son of a bitch—so darn heavy like a giant.*

Hirun gave up, and the night thus ticked away painfully.

## 6: Hirun and Beardy

The nephew was staring hard at the two uncles who seemed, uncannily, much happier than yesterday.

'What are you smiling for?'

'What?'

'What are YOU smiling for? It's giving me the creeps.'

'Oi, look at you. Who taught you to speak to adults like that?'

Even while chiding his nephew, Hirun was too elated to actually fight with Saeng. Beardy, too, laughed along.

Your writer is fully aware that she isn't too good at writing about love, as she lives in an era where dreams are robbed, the government is full of shit, and crises of faith happen on a daily basis. Due to all that, she is fully convinced that an everlasting love would only take place once one of them (or both) passed away.

Oh, there's no need to worry; no one dies in this story. But as I have just told you that your writer is an amateur at writing about lives after love comes true, she's now contemplating whether she should wrap up the story right here. Does anyone have any questions?

Will they be together?

Please allow me to give you a vague answer on this. Let's just say that Beardy has been going to 'The Tempest' for their fish sauce chicken wings more often after that. From then on, the young manager of the place has a new wager: 'If you win a game of Eight Ball against me, I'll tell Uncle to come see you. If not, give me cigarettes.' Beardy knows full well that regardless of the outcome, Hirun's nephew would go call his uncle for him anyway—the boy's actually much nicer than he makes himself out to be, so said Beardy. As for Saeng himself, he whispered to me that he simply didn't feel like listening to an old geezer's melancholic soliloquy in front of the piano as if the man has gotten his heart broken.

'And,' he added, 'it's high time Uncle has a hubby, so he'd stop following me around like a goldfish's string of poop at last.'

The boy was right. We are seeing less and less of the owner of 'The Tempest'. He brought out his old motorcycle and got its engine changed. It wasn't like he went and got a fancy exhaust system, but the motorcycle had been collecting dust for so long that the engine was no longer running. Thus, his expensive big bike gave a repair shop a visit and came back all gallant. He'd disappear three days at a time, oftentimes during the weekends with a public holiday lined up, considering how his sole companion was an office worker with limited vacation days. During those disappearances, he'd leave the keys to the place with his nephew who isn't yet of legal age, and this act of his wasn't the least bit applaudable in your writer's eyes. Oh, well. All employees at 'The Tempest' unanimously agree that the owner ought to have some days off at last, to which your writer agrees.

As for the future, Hirun isn't too certain of it and doesn't want to comment on it. Beardy has changed a lot in the past ten years that they were apart, but now that he gets to see the man more often, Hirun feels as if his friend's got more handsome. With one's youth gone, their taste will be more or less changed; there's no need for Beardy to look like a cool villain any more, as the one part of Beardy that Hirun likes is his pair of melancholic eyes that resemble a Wong Kar-wai's male lead. He doesn't have to wander about all dirty on his motorcycle any more either—Hirun much prefers the air-conditioned privacy of hotel rooms than those jam-packed shared dormitories in hostels.

Beardy, having gone through one failed marriage, is quite careful about matters concerning one's emotions. He later admitted to Hirun that he said he *liked* him because he didn't want Hirun to abandon him any more.

'I don't want to keep you hanging, but can we stay like this for now? You don't have anyone else that you like either, right? I'm not asking you to wait for me—I'm just . . .'

Right then, Hirun would knock Beardy hard on his head with his knuckles. 'I'm tired of this already. Come up with something new.' Then he would light a cigarette and hand Beardy one, and Beardy would light his cigarette from the glowing ember at the end of Hirun's cigarette, which would take quite a long while. Once Beardy would be comfortable in the embrace of the cigarette smoke, Hirun would lean closer to him and softly whisper, 'I'll wait, but make it quick.' Then, he would simply walk away.

That's when Beardy would come to the realization. He would run in front of Hirun, then grab his friend's hand. As for the event that follows, I'm certain that it won't be beyond my dear readers' ability to make a guess. And with that, I conclude this story here.

# Author's Note

**Two young boys in a small town, summer, a secret hideout, wishes, and nefarious plans.**

I wrote Juveniles just to satisfy some simple wishes: I wanted to write a story with a character with the personality of a loyal dog and the other, a mischievous troublemaker. The latter of which, of course, is Hai Saeng . . . But Hai Saeng isn't someone that would settle with something so bland, so he snatched my notepad and orchestrated this off-pitched song himself. He was standing right next to me as I typed the story away, whispering softly, 'Dig deep, go deeper, dig until you reach the pains from your juvenile days. If you're going to write about one bad child, then let's write them based on that secret you're too afraid to tell anyone about.'

That's the kind person Hai Saeng is—cruel.

Then I had to suffer through longer, more detailed chapters . . . Having to face a traumatic experience from your youth was quite hard on me. Once I reached the last part of the story, a reader left a comment on the website ReadAwrite: '*Hai Saeng's pain is so deeply rooted that I'm not sure whether anyone could come to terms with it within one lifetime.*' This spurred me to think about my own experience. I was a normal child who led a normal life due to how my brain made sure that I forgot about all painful memories, when in fact I'm a walking timebomb that's waiting for the world to fall apart once I grow up, once someone makes those memories resurface, and once everything I hold on to comes tumbling down in front of my eyes.

Returning to the question: have I come to terms with that traumatic experience? Well, I no longer feel pain recalling it, but I almost didn't survive going through the process, and the method I used wasn't to simply forgive in a Buddhist way like what Dao Nhue's mom teaches her child; it was to destroy everything to my heart's content, and slowly collect my broken self together with all those shattered things, put them back in place piece by piece, grab a brush to mend them together with glue, and gently fit the next piece into the gap. I tried to love myself so as to not hurt another, spent a year having nightmares, another visiting a psychologist, and two more years taking the medication before I was able to look back to the one who left me a grievous wound without any hostility.

As of today, I'm yet unable to say with confidence that I have forgiven them, and there's no need for me to. Down in the lake that resides within my heart, there lives yet a girl with a face void of emotions, a knife or perhaps a club clutched in her hand, with which she stabs and shatters everything into small pieces. Such aggressive and unruly behaviour might trouble my dear readers or leave them with a negative feeling towards certain characters, the writer, or make them feel concerned about the message that I'm trying to convey to the society.

But I beg you to believe me: To mend something, destruction is sometimes needed.

With love,
Moonscape, 2024